THE YOUNG DON'T THINK OF DEATH

By

Kevin Brandon

To Dublin, for all her faults and wonders.

To Anne

from
Johnny

CONTENTS

For Noel, George and Niall, whose wit inspired this book.

CHAPTER ONE

Business was dead, and then a corpse walked in.

There is a western city on a bay called Dublin. It's a low-rise city of more than a million people. There are both sexes in the city, and others who are not too sure. Every city in the world has its problems and Dublin is no different. It's my job to sort some of them out. My name is Jack Russell and I'm a private investigator.

The December afternoon was quiet, and my horses were falling at the first fence. It was the jump season and any good punter will tell you that bookies have the advantage over fences. Losing my shirt on bad jumpers was bad enough, but not getting a run for my money was something more serious.

I had a small two-room office on City Quay overlooking the River Liffey, near where it enters the bay. Until the collapse, they'd been tarting up the docklands, cleaning them up and building new apartments and office blocks. That was the time of the Celtic Tiger when the politicians swore blind that the good times would last forever. However, politicians have been known to tell fibs on occasion. Then the property market had taken a nosedive and prices were falling faster than rain in the Amazon basin. The confidence fled the city like refugees from a war zone. From my window I could see the skeletons of former dreams across the river, unfinished monuments to failed vanity.

There was an unfinished bank amongst the skeletons, its grey concrete shell rising up like the bones of a dead dinosaur. The bank was broke, living on a life-support system backed up by the taxpayer. That's how it is in Ireland: the taxpayer always picks up the bill.

Another of my horses fell at the first fence and I turned off the small overhead TV. The office was in an old brick building that once had been a corn warehouse. Somehow it had escaped the grasping clutches of the builders and the pinstriped property tycoons during the collective madness of the Celtic Tiger. The office was on the ground floor because my secretary didn't like climbing stairs. She suffered from acrophobia and various other ailments.

Her name was Jane Hackett, but she's married now with another name. Jane was big into colours. She often wore her hair dyed an extreme shade of pink. That dyed hair was not good for business, but it went with the territory of the young. Apart from that pink hair and the acrophobia, she was not a bad secretary.

It was Friday afternoon, snow falling, and the day was not getting any better. Darkness loomed outside in a pall, lying low over the grey city and river. I wrote out an each-way bet for Slippery Sam in the next race. The odds were ridiculous, but I had to get my money back somehow. The desk phone rang to interrupt my thoughts.

"Want the good news or the bad news?"

"Let's get the bad stuff out of the way."

"The next race has been cancelled."

"At Fairyhouse?"

"It's snowed off. I heard it on the radio. The bookies won't be getting any more of your money today, Jack. Besides, you should not be gambling today. It's Friday the thirteenth. It took all my willpower to get out of bed this morning."

"What's the good news?"

"You get to keep your shirt."

"Get off the stage, Jane."

I made a phone call to my landlord, Jim Piggot. He had a smile like a beacon and a wallet that hadn't seen the light of day in a year. There was a toilet downstairs that could have been used for storing meat. An Eskimo couldn't use it because of the cold. It didn't flush properly either. He had promised to put a heater on the wall and fix the toilet. He'd done neither.

"I can't get tradesmen," he lied.

"I thought there was a property crash here. There should be plenty of them on the dole."

"All emigrated."

"What about that reduction in rent, Jim? I'm still paying Celtic Tiger prices here."

"Insurance costs haven't dropped."

I hung up and went to the window. My watch said it was approaching four, but it had often lied before. I opened the window and lit up a cigarette. A cold blast of air sent the smoke in wisps around the office. Jane loved smokers like a rabbit loves a fox. I threw it out the window and returned to the desk.

That's when the corpse walked in. It wasn't an assumption on my part because she told me she was dead. She was aged in her early or mid-thirties, and she wore black. Her face was grey, and she had the look of death about her. However, the laws of life and death state that the dead can't walk. They can't talk either, and she had walked and talked.

"Can you read?"

"Yes," she said.

Her voice was low, but she was talking. She told me she was dead. My eyes are not twenty-twenty, but I could see up to fifty paces, and she was closer than that. She was alive, as far as I could tell. I pushed my desk diary under her nose. It was grey; her nose, not the diary.

"Read what it says at the top of the page."

"Friday, December thirteen."

"Right, not April first."

"You think this is some sort of joke, Jack?"

"Unless there's a Second Coming I haven't heard about."

Now she sat. Her hands were pale, deathly white against her dress. I couldn't make out the colour of her eyes because a black veil covered them. She was looking at me intensely.

I tried to figure out how she knew my name. It

wasn't written up on the front door. You don't write your name up where you'll be thrown out when property values rise.

"Okay, I'll go along."

I had time on my hands to listen. It was a good act. She had gone to a lot of trouble to grab my attention. My thoughts weren't on sunny places because at this rate I couldn't afford a holiday. There was no wife waiting at home for me either, so I had nothing better to do than listen.

"You don't believe me, Jack. You have heard of Lazarus?"

"Sure, I backed him at Cheltenham. Fell at the third."

"Do you require proof?"

She unbuttoned her dress, starting from the neck. She had a black bra, stark against the grey skin. Her breasts were like two prisoners trying to escape from a cage. She undid the bra, and set them free. They were grey too, the colour of death. Between her breasts was a black hole. It appeared to have had been made by a bullet.

"Thomas doubted too, Jack. Do you wish to put your finger in the wound? Well? It can't hurt me because I'm dead,"

My head indicated no. She buttoned up again. Her gaze was fixed on me behind the veil. Now she had my full attention. The races and foolish dreams of getting my money back were put away. My mind was fully focussed.

"Look, what's this charade all about? By the way,

do you have a name? Or do the dead have names?"

"Murphy, Mrs Colleen Murphy."

She had no rings on her grey finger. That's the first thing a bachelor notices in a woman. Well, maybe not.

"How'd you get my name?"

"The dead know everything, Jack."

I was going to ask for the winner of the next race, until I remembered Fairyhouse was cancelled. Outside the window snow drifted lazily down. The bookies were offering even money on a white Christmas. It had to be a better bet than the horses.

The downturn had thrown some business my way. I did a lot of work for insurance companies. They paid me to find out if a woman claiming for a broken back was lapdancing at weekends to supplement her income. You'd be surprised how many cripples were out playing football on a Sunday morning with broken legs before going to the pub for a rake of pints. But I'd never had a corpse for a client before.

Maybe corpses felt the cold too. The electric heater behind the desk had one bar lighting. I flicked a switch and the second bar came on. I'd been meaning to get a gas heater but it kept slipping my mind.

"What do they use for money in the afterlife? I charge four hundred euro a day and five for Saturdays and Sundays. The rent here is high and I have a secretary to pay which explains the fees. I try to keep Sundays free if possible, unless it's urgent. I don't charge for food and drink, but bribes are extra. It's not enough to live in the Ritz, but it helps me get by."

"Bribes?"

"They have a way of getting things done."

From somewhere she produced a wad of notes. There was a few grand in it at least. The money had no soil attached, and it didn't smell. It looked good enough to pass for real. Maybe she had taken it with her, despite the priests saying you can't.

"Consider that a retainer, Jack."

"How do I earn this, Mrs Murphy?"

"Colleen, please."

"How do I earn this, Colleen?"

Despite everything, I found myself thinking normally. Her accent was hard to place, but I could tell she didn't come from the inner city. It was sort of neutral, hard to pin down. But it was an educated accent. It had cost somebody a lot of money to give her that accent. It was foreign, except her English was perfect.

"My husband murdered me."

I thought how easy life would be if the dead could talk.

No killers walking free. No miscarriages of justice. Nobody locked up who should be out walking the streets. One hundred percent murder clear-up rate. But the dead don't talk. They can't talk because they're dead.

"Hasn't this gone far enough?"

She opened up the wad of notes. At the centre of the wad was a press clipping. She pushed it across the desk. A year back the wife of a prominent barrister had been murdered, shot in the chest. The murder had made headline news because they were important people. The people of no importance who got themselves murdered didn't rate the first page. They got a small paragraph on the inside if they were lucky.

She was dressed in a stylish gown of dark pink. They were at a premiere of a movie filmed in the city, the sort of bash that all the important people attended. There was a man at her side, Paul Murphy. He was a barrister who specialised in keeping rich clients out of prison, white collar criminals. Planning corruption, kickbacks to politicians and local authority officials, money laundering, that sort of thing. Murphy was a great one for human rights. If one of his clients was found with ten million euro in an offshore bank account, he'd claim the matter couldn't be investigated since it might infringe his client's human rights. In his world the victims of white collar crime had no human rights, and didn't deserve any either. They were suckers who deserved to be cleaned out.

"That's my husband, Jack. He murdered me."

She pulled the veil from her eyes. I compared her to the picture on the press cutting. There was a likeness. The dead are different, but there was a striking similarity. Same eyes, same blue. My head couldn't figure it out.

"Now do you believe me?"

"Why not go to the cops?"

"And get this reception from them?"

A good point. I studied the picture again. Her hair was piled high on her head, Greek style. It was brown in the picture, and it was brown in my office. Except now she wore it plain and falling to her shoulders. Apart from the deathly complexion, she was the woman in the picture. There was no doubt in my mind. And yet a voice inside insisted that the dead do not come back. That was contrary to every known law.

"Will you take the case, Jack?"

The phone rang. It was the landlord looking for his rent. I was still smarting over the previous conversation. Celtic Tiger rents in a bloody downturn! He had a bloody cheek. I walked to the window because I had to use words I didn't want a corpse to hear. Swearing has way of upsetting live people. Maybe swear words might upset the dead too.

"No fucken toilet, no heat, and you want fucken rent?"

"Watch the language, I'm a practising Christian."

"What about the commandment against fucken theft?"

"I can have another client in there in a week."

"There are not that many masochists, even in Ireland."

So we argued for a few minutes. My language echoed my frustration. He was pleading poverty. He had a wife and kids. He pointed out I had neither. I said his wife and kids were his problem, not mine. As usual, it ended in stalemate. When I turned around, the corpse was gone.

"Jane, come in here a minute."

Jane was a multi-tasker. She could chew gum and paint her nails at the same time. At that time the nails were blue, but it was a temporary condition. I'd seen better nails, but only in the movies and they're usually false. She examined them with the eye of an expert of the subject. She seemed satisfied with the result and her eyes.

"Did you see the woman who just left?"

"A client? Don't exaggerate, Jack."

"She left this wad of notes on the desk."

"Where'd you get that? I thought Fairyhouse was off."

"I didn't win it…"

"No need to tell me that."

"Stop chewing and painting, and listen. A woman came in here dressed in black and gave me that. She was here for at least ten minutes. Did you see her?"

I thought it best not to mention she was dead.

"No woman came in here, Jack."

"Resembling a corpse?"

"I could recommend a good optician, Jack. A man of your age should be wearing glasses. Want me to count that?"

"I'm not blind yet."

Jane left, still painting and chewing. I was left in a state of bewilderment. My mind returned to the corpse. Colleen Murphy had class, even for a dead woman. I suspected she'd been to a fancy finishing school, probably in Switzerland. And class is the only commodity that can't be taught. They don't bottle it either so you can't buy it off the shelf. You either have it or you don't.

I counted the notes. There was five grand in the wad, made up of fifties. The office turned darker and I switched on the light.

The sky had turned a murkier shade of grey, with huge ominous clouds hovering over the city. No sign of the sun. Snow was falling in soft drifts. Winter is not my favourite time of year. I prefer summer with the sun high in the sky, and the days long and hot. That's why I holidayed in Spain, business permitting. Except I hadn't been to any Costa in three years.

I had a mobile phone. It couldn't tell the time in Beijing, or the exchange rate in Hong Kong. But it could tell the time in Dublin, and receive a call. It could also take a picture, very useful in my job. It rang in tones, and I recognised the voice.

"How'd you get this number?"

"The dead know everything, Jack. I need help. Are you ready to help me? I am no crank. Are the funds sufficient?"

"I think you need a psychiatrist, not a private eye."

"I'm quite sane, Jack."

I checked my diary for the week. It was emptier than a bucket with no bottom. On my desk there was a souvenir bull from my last holiday, and an ashtray. I put the ashtray in a drawer to avoid flak from Jane. Overhead on a shelf was a small TV, and on the floor a waste basket filled with yesterday's betting slips. There was not a winner in there. Not one. I thought my luck had to change soon.

Then, in an instant, I felt lower than a snake's belly. She started to cry over the phone. I could hear floods of tears fall from her eyes.

I could sense her body shaking like a leaf in a gale. That always gets to a man, a woman crying.

"Okay, okay, just stop crying."

"Can we meet tonight?"

"Sure. Where?"

"The Hole-In-The-Wall pub in the Park?"

"Sure. Say eight?"

"Ten would be better."

I knew the pub. Situated at the Phoenix Park, it was dark and discreet. It had private areas where it was possible to talk. A lot of Dublin pubs had lost that. The Celtic Tiger had swept quietness in pubs away like a hurricane over an island. Blaring music is no substitute for banter in a pub.

I was there an hour early and sipped a pint. I reckoned one pint wouldn't put me over the limit. The recession had taken its toll on pubs too. A few casual drinkers were there, but no crowds, even for a Friday night. She was on time, and asked for a coffee, black, no milk or sugar. She was still dressed in black, and her pale complexion hadn't changed.

"You want proof, Jack?" she said.

She took a small plastic phial from somewhere. She had one of those things for cleaning out a baby's ears, like a matchstick with cotton wool on the end. She ran it around her mouth a few times and put it in the phial. I'd seen this sort of thing on TV. It was a way of collecting DNA.

"There is your proof, Jack. Now, pluck a few

strands of hair from my head. What's the matter? I won't mind. It can't hurt worse than a bullet in the chest. A bullet hurts, especially when fired by the man who was my husband."

So I plucked a few strands of hair and put them in the phial.

She didn't react. The phial went into my pocket.

"He murdered me because he was having an affair, several in fact," she began, as if talking about the latest soap opera. "Of course I demanded a divorce. I believe fidelity is the cornerstone of a true marriage. Naturally he refused to give me a divorce."

"Why naturally?"

"Ireland has changed. Some years ago, he could have dumped me and kept everything. Now I'm entitled to half of everything he owns. Some judges would give me the majority of his possessions because I kept my marriage vows. I didn't care about his money, I just wanted enough to live on."

I took out a note book and pen. "Do you have the name of his mistress? Her address?"

"We are talking in the plural here, Jack."

"I see. Any of them?"

"Unfortunately not."

"How'd you know he had mistresses?"

"Because I'm not stupid."

Okay, so she was smart, but the dead didn't know everything.

Colleen Murphy sipped the coffee in the manner

of a queen. She didn't slurp, and she had a way of holding the cup that could have gotten her a job in the diplomatic corps at the Vatican. I reckoned she'd been taught how to hold a cup in that fancy Swiss finishing school for young ladies with rich families. Maybe that's where she'd picked up the cultured accent. The way she sat on the pub chair too, with her legs folded under it, proved that she had learned the art of composure. I'm told by people who know about these things that composure needs a lot of practice to get right.

"Give me the names of his friends and hangouts."

She gave me names and I wrote them down. She gave me the name of his golf club and other venues he frequented to be seen and get his pictures in the newspapers. A celebrity lawyer needs publicity and exposure too, just like every other celebrity.

I filled a couple of pages with the names. She had a good memory, even if she didn't know the names of his multiple mistresses.

"I hope you don't mind me calling you Jack."

"That's my name, Jack Russell."

"Why did you choose this line of work?"

She didn't make the obvious remark. I liked her for that. She didn't say my name sounded like a breed of dog, as if I had chosen the name for myself. She had a slow way of saying my name that made me feel the most important man in the world. I sensed the hair rising on the back of my neck. There was something about her that brought out the protector in me. Sure, I wanted to help her. Then I begin to think about her husband. He was still making the front pages, for the wrong reasons.

"It seemed a good idea at the time."

"And now?"

"It pays the bills, sometimes. I'll need some details about your husband. His home and office addresses, where he goes for his holidays, who works for him — that sort of thing."

"Don't you read the gossip pages in the Sunday papers?"

"*The Racing Post* is more my style."

"I see. Gambling is a weakness."

"Not when my horse passes the post first."

"How often does that happen?

"Last time it happened was November the thirtieth."

She proceeded to list his addresses and employee. He had a secretary who worked his office. He did have loads of friends. People with his sort of money usually had the sort of friends that are impressed by the stuff. However, when I asked for her address she was silent. It was a simple request. I hadn't asked for the number of her bank account, but her address seemed more important.

"How do I contact you?"

"I'll contact you," she said.

She handed me a picture of their wedding day. She wore white and he wore black. She was about five years younger then, maybe thirty. He was a few years older. He had the look of a professional man with no worries about money, or the future. Worry was for other people, not for a man on his way to the top of a legal firm.

You can tell a lot from a photograph, especially one in colour. It was Paris, with the Eiffel Tower in the background. They were laughing into the camera. There was no photograph of the hotel where the reception was held, but it had to be five stars plus. No expense had been spared that day. I might have remembered the occasion except I read the *Racing Post* instead of the gossip pages in the Sunday newspapers.

"Can I hold onto this?"

"Of course, Jack."

"What model car does he drive?"

"Depends. A Mercedes for work, a Range Rover for leisure. He also has a vintage MGB in the garage that he's restoring. Well, a mechanic is restoring it for him. He attends rallies for petrolheads. He tells them he's restoring the car himself but he wouldn't know the basic difference between a crankshaft and a carburettor."

"Do you?"

"Yes. Cars are a speciality of mine."

No recession in the legal profession. Peculiar how some professions always ride out recessions, the ones associated with the law. She had a good head for numbers, and I scribbled down the plate numbers of the cars. Then I put away the notebook in my inside pocket. I needed to be careful with my next words.

"Can you talk about your...?"

"My murder? Why are you afraid to use the word?"

"I never had to ask a corpse before."

"It was Christmas Eve, last year. I was preparing dinner. We had two servants, but they had gone away for Christmas, out of the country. Paul was late. He was due home at seven, after a few drinks with friends after work."

"Work? On Christmas Eve?"

"Same here. It was a euphemism for going to a club with his friends. Strange how a man with no morality can have friends, isn't it? Birds of a feather, obviously. He probably went to one of those lap-dancing joints. Have you attended any?"

"I can't dance."

"I'm told the girls do the dancing."

"I'll take your word on it. You were alone in the house?"

"Yes. I cooked dinner, *coq au vin.*"

"What's that?"

"A sort of French stew with wine. Anyway, he arrived home an hour later, at eight. He seemed in good form. I was in the kitchen when I saw the gun in his hand. I shall never forget the look on his face. He wore a smile, but I hadn't seen him use it before. He shot me once only in the chest with an old gun. Then he bundled me into the car and took me for a ride. He drove to the Wicklow Mountains and left me there at the wheel. I was dead, of course."

"What make of car?"

"My car. A Ford Focus."

"How'd he get back to the house?"

"No idea."

He hadn't taken a taxi, that's for sure. The cops would have rung the taxi firms to check. Maybe he'd had an accomplice, someone to pick him up. Maybe he'd arranged it with one of his mistresses. It wouldn't be the first time a mistress assisted in the murder of her lover's wife. It never seemed to occur to them that they could be next.

We went for a stroll in the park afterwards. Scatterings of snow were strewn on the grass. The night sky was clear, and the streetlamps cast us in shadows. I can't recall what we talked about. It seemed natural because I didn't allow logic to interfere with the walk. She left me there under the night sky, and walked away into the darkness.

CHAPTER TWO

David Lanigan was a stockbroker who wanted to talk about investments in futures, whatever that was. I didn't think the future could be bought but he was selling it anyway. We met in Wynn's Hotel in Abbey Street for lunch. He was getting a free lunch and I was expecting answers. I'd phoned him up and asked about investing money with him. I knew he wouldn't have met me otherwise.

I had to dress for the part so I wore a suit and tie instead of the usual sweater and open-neck shirt. He was one of her husband's friends, and she'd given me his name and phone number. Lanigan was thirty to forty with dark crewcut hair and glasses. He looked as if he still played rugby for the right school. He said genetic crops were the future. He gave me the sales pitch as if he believed the story himself. They were banned in Europe, but the Americans would get their way as usual and force them on us. There were trials going down about free trade between Europe and America. Trade was more important than health concerns. Trade trumped everything according to him.

"It's good business," he said.

"Not Frankenstein food?"

He shot up, as if kicked in the nuts. "Of course not! All these tree-hugging fucken faggots make me mad! There is not enough food in the world. It's a sound investment. Have you any idea of the opportunities here? It's the place to be."

"So Paul Murphy tells me."

He dabbed his lips with a napkin. "You a friend of his? I don't seem to recall his mentioning your name."

"I met him a few times at vintage car rallies. I have an old Triumph Stag, redone engine and gearbox. It's a hobby of mine. Some men play golf. He mentioned you when we chewed the fat over old cars. Last time we met he said you had a good piss-up last Christmas Eve."

I was fishing, and he took the bait.

"What a day! We went a pub crawl that day. Ended up in a Chinese whorehouse down in Marlborough Street, a high-class joint, none of your riff-raff allowed. Do you know they have a menu for all their services just like a restaurant? All the politicians and judges go there. Guess the best part?"

Lanigan was a true cub of the Celtic Tiger. He had not lost any of the hubris of that era. It was business as usual. He was much the same as a Bourbon king. He had learned nothing, or forgotten nothing.

"What's the best part?"

"We claimed it on expenses! They front as a restaurant, so a ride can be put down as a meal. And you can claim for a meal on expenses, if you have a good accountant. It's the way to go, man."

"How many of you were there?"

"Three of us, the three amigos. There was me, and Paul, and Philip Grogan. He has a big law firm down on Wellington Quay. What a day! No wives to nag us."

"Paul is a great character. When did you break up?"

"Let me see, we left the whorehouse at six, and then did a pub crawl until a quarter to eight. Fifteen minutes later we put Paul in a taxi. Man, was he out of it! I recall looking at my watch in the taxi rank. The journey to his home takes forty minutes on a good night. On Christmas Eve it would have taken much longer, maybe twice that. I took a taxi home myself."

"That was the night his wife was killed?"

"Sure," he nodded. "The fucken bitch. She wanted to take him to the cleaners because he was having fun. Show me the man who doesn't sleep around and I'll show you a closet homo. A wife should be grateful to have a real man for her husband. Too much of that LGBT stuff in this country for my liking."

"Who do you think killed her?"

"Who cares? She deserved it."

He wanted to talk about selling me the future. I was more interested in the past. I asked if he had a card for the joint down on Marlborough Street. He was happy to oblige, and told me to mention his name. I promised to call him later, but the air outside smelled nicer than his company. An abattoir would have smelled nicer than his company.

Philip Grogan wasn't seeing anybody. I was in his offices down on Wellington Quay. Business was booming, with a list of clients seated on plush sofas ready to see him. I knew then I was in the wrong line of work. It wasn't the first time either. His receptionist lied through a smile of pearly white teeth that indicated she attended a good dentist. She said he was at court.

I happened to know the courts worked union hours. I requested an appointment. The receptionist promised to make one. I left his offices, but I wasn't holding my breath.

When a wife is murdered, the husband is always number one suspect. It works the other way too, although more wives are murdered than husbands. The cops would have checked out his alibi with a firehose. It had to be watertight. It had to be tighter than a duck's anus in winter. There are few things tighter than a duck's anus.

Her number wasn't coming up on my phone. I was leaving the office on Wellington Quay when it rang. She had to be calling from a public phone somewhere. Public phones were rare in the city, superseded by new technology. I wondered why she wasn't using a mobile phone when kids as young as five were.

"Where is your car now, Colleen?"

"The Ford? I don't know. Why?"

"The cops probably have it locked up somewhere. I'll find out. I can't get to see Philip Grogan. He's ignoring me. I must be using the wrong aftershave."

"Didn't I give you his home address?"

"Sure, but he has a wife and children. I don't feel the need to drag them into this. His wife would ask questions if I turned up at the house asking questions about her husband's choice of friends and social life. She's done nothing wrong."

"You are right, of course."

"That Christmas Eve when your husband was late? Did you phone around to find out where he was?"

"I phoned the office, but of course it was closed. I phoned his golf club, but he wasn't there. I phoned his local pub, but he wasn't there. I also phoned several hospitals. Why?"

A man is late home on Christmas Eve in Dublin, and his wife is worried. That sort of thing happens all the time. It's not news. News is when something unusual happens, like a married man dancing with his wife on O'Connell Street in Dublin. But that night the wife of the man was murdered. Now that is news.

"Well, it showed you cared, Colleen."

She didn't talk about children. I suspected she had none, and I didn't ask. I went to an Internet café near the river and had a cup of coffee. The waitress showed me how to use the computer.

She found the murder online, and let me browse. It's strange how an event shocks the memory at first, but soon fades. The murder had been on everyone's lips a year ago, and now nobody talked about it. I read the details:

'Mister Paul Murphy, the eminent barrister, arrived home by taxi on Christmas Eve at nine o'clock with a present for his wife, Colleen. He had been dining with friends and colleagues, and afterwards had gone to a pub for a few drinks. He drank two small brandies only, but had decided to take a taxi home rather than drive. He had found his home eerily silent, with no sign of his wife. Her car was missing, which had not alarmed him at first. Perhaps she had forgotten something from the shops, and had gone to fetch it. He noticed that the dinner was still simmering on the cooker. It was *coq au vin*. He had watched TV for an hour, until becoming worried. He had made numerous phone calls to the hospitals and to the guards thinking perhaps she'd been involved in an accident. But his wife seemed to have vanished from the face of the earth. Three days later her body was found in her car by a walker in the Wicklow Mountains. The guards have ruled out robbery as a motive, since she was wearing the expensive gold chain her husband had given her for Christmas.'

The newspapers could only speculate on the reason for her murder. Some suggested a liaison with a lover, since the dead can't be libelled. However, her friends denied she'd been having an affair. She had, they said, lived for her husband. I tended to believe her friends rather than the speculations.

Sarah Corbally was renovating an old artisan house near Cork Street when I called. She wore a smock with paint splotches, and a bump. She glanced at my card and asked who I was working for. I told her it was an insurance company. She said her husband was at work and invited me inside. The place was in bits. Strips of old wallpaper streamed from the walls like ribbons. Some floorboards were missing so I had to pick my steps.

"Did that bastard claim insurance? After he murdered her?"

"Not yet. He won't claim when he's still a suspect."

"I hope he rots in jail. But he's rich. The rich don't get jail in this bloody country for murder. They buy their way out. They buy the best solicitors."

"He is a solicitor."

"I know, and they're as thick as thieves."

She was angry. Colleen had been her friend. I had seen her grieving on the Internet. She'd been powerless to do anything about the murder. She could rant at the moon like a wolf and it wouldn't have mattered. That's why she mouthed off to me. She had to get if off her chest.

"What can you tell me about Colleen Murphy?"

"I met her fifteen years ago, and we hit it off. We both worked in a department store. We did everything together – pubs, concerts. Then she went to work for a politician as his personal assistant. She was always interested in politics, unlike me. She changed after that, becoming more ambitious, but we kept in touch. What do you think of ambition, Mr Russell?"

"My lifestyle answers that question."

"Too many people get hurt by ambition. Why do people admire ambition? It should be condemned. All I ever wanted was a home I could afford, and a man to love me."

"What about her family?"

"She came originally from Carlow, from a small village called Saint Mullins. It's beautiful down there, but she used to say you can't eat the scenery. So she headed to the bright lights. She was only thirty-five when he murdered her. Imagine that. Sorry, what was the question?"

"Had she any family?"

"She had no kids. Her mother died shortly after she came to Dublin. I attended the funeral with her. Her father died when she was very young. She had no brothers and sisters. That's why she regarded me as the sister she never had."

"Her maiden name? Any boyfriends?"

"Dowling was her maiden name. She had no boyfriends before she met her killer. Nothing serious. She met him at a political rally. She introduced me to him. You know, I never did take to him. A creepy chill went up my spine when he was around. He was…he is a *mefeiner,* one of those men who care only for themselves. I tried to talk her out of marrying him, but she wouldn't listen."

I had never met Paul Murphy, but I knew he was one of those men, a mefeiner, only out for himself. Those sorts of men attracted others with the same character.

"When are you due?"

"Oh, this?" she said, patting her tummy. "April."

"Apparently he has a cast-iron alibi for that night."

"Why not? His sort always have alibis. They can buy any amount of alibis. He's a member of the Law Society too, a closed club. Those people take care of their own. He's not from the inner city after all."

"Oh, I almost forgot, what type of education did Colleen have? Was she sent abroad?"

"Abroad?" she said, shaking her head. "Her father was a brickie. Her mother was a secretary. Colleen was educated in a local primary school, same as the rest of us. Her parents could not afford her a college education."

"You certain? It's important."

"Sure I'm certain."

That didn't fit with the corpse who called herself Colleen Murphy. She had been educated to a high standard. She had been taught how to drink tea and how to sit properly. Drinking tea is easily taught but how to sit correctly all the time without fluffing your lines is much more difficult. Maybe she had taught herself how to sit with legs folded and feet beneath the chair. People of ambition often do.

"That her?" I asked, showing the paper clipping.

"Yes, that's Colleen."

"Why do you think he killed her?"

"He's too calculating to be a psychopath. There is no doubt in my mind why he killed her. Colleen was going through a rough patch in her marriage, and confided in me. I advised her to divorce him. A month before her murder she phoned to say she was going to divorce him. That's why he murdered her, to keep everything for himself."

It was the oldest motive in the book, and had not lost its appeal. Money motivates like nothing else. It has the power to do anything. Jealousy is not even in the same league. It doesn't take a crystal ball to see that a thousand years into the future husbands will still be murdering their wives for money.

"Had he a replacement wife lined up?"

"More than likely, but she never said."

"No suggestions?"

"Probably someone from his own circle."

Now I showed her the wedding photograph in Paris. She winced, but said it was the same Colleen. She herself had been the bridesmaid, except she wasn't in the picture. I kept looking at it as if trying to find something amiss, something that might offer a clue to the murder. They both seemed genuinely happy. Yet something had driven the groom to murder his wife whom he had vowed to love for eternity.

"They seem very happy in that picture."

"No bride frowns on her wedding day, Mr Russell."

"As my card says, I work for an insurance company and get a bonus when they don't have to pay out. Any name you could give me that might help? The car needs a lot of work and I could do with the bonus. I'd much appreciate it."

"Anything to stop that vulture from feeding off her corpse. Have you heard of Darren Pringle? He does be on TV a lot. He's a fashion guru, you know, the type who's famous for being famous. He's a famous bungalow, you know, nothing on top. He was always around the killer."

Pringle told women how to dress, and was paid for the privilege. He was paid to judge fashion at race meetings, but only on the flat. Jump racing has few fashion shows. He was a celebrity because he could talk about fashion in a serious voice. Don't ask me to explain why a fashion guru can become a celebrity, but Pringle was. He wrote a weekly column about what to wear, and he appeared regularly on afternoon TV with similar ladies. He had a good smile, and a better line in chat. He didn't discuss the meaning of life on afternoon TV shows, but then nobody expected him to talk about that to an afternoon audience.

"How do I get to meet him?"

"He has a shop in Grafton Street."

I drove back to my comfortable office through slushy streets and dreams of Marbella. I politely asked Jane to find out everything she could about Murphy & Associates, the law firm owned by Paul Murphy. She didn't even reply. But when I asked her to find out about Darren Pringle her eyes lit brighter than a fireworks display in China for the New Year.

"He's a celebrity, Jack. Why investigate him?"

"If I don't, you don't get paid."

"But celebrities don't do nothing wrong, Jack."

"No? Ever see the hats he designs for race days?"

"What the fuck do you know about fashion?"

Jane was looking at her reflected image in a mirror and painting her nails at the same time. She could also type whilst reading the gossip column. It was amazing that she never made a typing error. I couldn't figure that out, but it wasn't the only thing about her I couldn't figure out. She was young and I put my lack of understanding down to that. She picked out a photograph of Darren Pringle. I said he looked like Art Garfunkel. She wanted to know who that was.

"So, this is what real money looks like?" she

commented, after I handed her the wad. She held a fifty to the pale winter light streaming in the window. "I was beginning to think it was going out of fashion. It's so long since I've seen it that I was thinking they'd abolished the stuff. It should keep the landlord off our backs for a couple of months."

Jane was from the north side of the city, across the Liffey. They are very witty on the north side. At least they think so. They're very proud of their funny heritage on the north side.

"How old do you think he is, Jack?"

"Pringle? Hard to tell with all the facelifts."

CHAPTER THREE

The offices of Murphy & Associates a were located on Church Street opposite Christchurch Cathedral. It was a modern townhouse with a fake Georgian exterior that had been converted into an office block with three floors. There was a polished brass plaque on the outside with the name. I rang the doorbell a couple of times before getting a response. Then I heard a voice over an intercom.

"Murphy & Associates. State your business."

With a welcome like that, I didn't feel bad about lying.

"I'm here on behalf of the late Mrs Colleen Murphy."

That threw the intercom for a minute or two. "Her grieving husband is taking care of that."

"Her grieving husband is number one suspect. I am here on behalf of her grieving relatives. I'm grieving too because I'm standing out here like an idiot. You'll be grieving too if you don't admit me because the law is on my side."

"She had no living relatives."

"I didn't realise intercoms were experts on families."

"Mrs Murphy had no relatives," the intercom insisted.

"There was a will, and this is Ireland. Where there's a will in this country, there are always relatives. It's the law that every dead person must leave behind living relatives whether they have any or not. Now, do I get in or do I have to go to the cops? I'm no good at talking to doors or having a conversation with an intercom."

"State your name."

"Jack Russell, and I'm a man."

The door clicked open and I went inside. The office was modest and sober, no doubt to infer honesty. It had a fawn carpet on the floor and sombre paint on the walls. A few portraits in watercolours painted romantic scenes of old Dublin. A receptionist or secretary sat behind a desk in the centre of the room. She was caressing her hands on a computer like a drummer playing fast jazz.

"Is Mister Paul Murphy in?" I asked.

"State your business."

"I already did on several occasions."

"What relatives are you representing?"

"Sorry, I didn't realise you were Paul Murphy. I had assumed he was male and you're female. My eyes are not the best but I can still tell the difference between a man and a woman. If I'm in error, do try to forgive me."

Her name was Anne Neary. I knew that because it was printed on a nameplate on her desk. She wore a white blouse and a grey skirt. The glasses were horn-rimmed, and give her a matronly appearance. She wasn't a dowdy woman, but she was working on it. For some reason, she appeared to like it that way. Anne had an attitude that came with the appearance. She was young, no more than thirty, but wore dated clothes and hair parted down the middle. Most women try to appear younger than their age but she was different.

"Mister Murphy is not here at present."

"I'll wait."

"Are you from the police?"

I handed her the card. She wasn't impressed. It had no gold lettering or fancy script. It was white with black letters, giving my name and occupation. It also had my telephone number and place of work. It didn't have my mobile number or home address because I like to separate work from leisure.

Her phone rang. She said 'Sir' a few times. It didn't take a genius to figure out she was talking to Murphy. She didn't even blush when she said I could go up and see him.

"Your nose will grow if you keep telling lies," I said.

Anyone who says first impressions don't count is a liar. My first impression of Paul Murphy was not a good one. He had that sense of superiority that comes with a man who believes he's above the law. It was an assumption on my part, but a good one. People who deal in the law think it doesn't apply to them. The law is for little people.

Paul Murphy sat in a high leather chair behind an oak desk with a commanding view of the city. He was a tallish man, not unlike his photograph in the wedding picture. The death of his wife hadn't put a single grey hair in his neatly cut black hair. He wore a shirt and a pair of gold cufflinks. His features were clean-cut, and were used to sway reluctant juries. There was no photograph of his wife on the desk.

"I am not a hypocrite," he stated.

"I said nothing."

"No, but you were looking for a photograph of my wife. We did not get on, that's why there is no photograph. But I did not kill her. Is that why you're here?"

"Murder is way above my pay scale. I do insurance work, that sort of thing. It's small stuff, so I'm thinking of going after bigger fish. You know the sort, fat bankers who brought down the country and didn't end up in jail. Speculators who borrowed millions and pleaded poverty when asked to pay it back. They're living in the Bahamas now, but the suckers who pay their taxes have to foot the bill."

We understood each other then.

The cigar he puffed was fatter than a blimp. It was Cuban.

I couldn't recall if there was a trade embargo on Cuba. I made a mental note to read better newspapers on Sundays. Murphy glanced at his watch to let me know his time was expensive, and so was the watch. He was wearing at least a grand of gold on his body, and that wasn't including the watch. He dressed to impress. The gold watch and expensive clothes also sent out a message that he was rich in his own right. He hadn't needed to murder his wife for money, but could have paid her off if she'd wanted to divorce him. I wasn't buying the message.

He asked for a card and I obliged. The college he'd attended had taught him to read. He examined the card as if it was a legal piece of evidence. It didn't impress him either. A smile crossed his tanned face. It had taken money to get that tan during winter in Ireland.

"Aren't you in the wrong place, Jack?"

"Is that a philosophical question?"

"No," he giggled. "Shouldn't you be at Crufts in London? I'm certain with your looks and pedigree that you'd win best of breed. A place in the history books beckon if you take the next plane and jet over there. Wouldn't that be better than wasting your time here?"

"It's my time to waste."

"Jack Russell," he laughed. "Your parents must have had a great sense of humour. Well, that's made my day."

"My father's name was Russell and my mother's name was Jack. I'm named after them both. I'd like to ask you about your wife, the late Mrs Colleen Murphy. It won't take long. If you can get past my name I'll be out of here in a few minutes."

"On whose behalf?"

"That is confidential."

"She had no living relatives. Besides, the insurance money is minimal. The relatives, if she has any, are welcome to it. Just give me their names and I'll take it from there. Will that be all?"

"Can you explain your movements the night she died?"

"Frankly, that is none of your fucken business."

"I see you attended the best legal colleges."

"There is the door. Close it behind you."

"Some people say you murdered your wife."

"Repeat that and I will sue your ass off."

"Some people say you murdered your wife. Ever hear of Happy Days in Marlborough Street?"

His guard dropped, but only for a second. He soon wheeled it back in line. Years at court had taught him not to show emotion. In a nanosecond his composure had returned.

"No, and the interview is over."

"Except you lied to the cops, Paul. They don't like a man who lies to them. They think he has something to hide. They think he's the type who kills his wife. If you lied under oath, that constitutes perjury. Sorry for pointing out the law to you but it's supposed to be impartial."

I knew he'd lied to the cops. He wasn't the type to admit to visiting a brothel. I had him now, like a salmon on a strong line. He'd co-operate in future, just to find out what I knew that he didn't. Of course, he wouldn't tell me the truth. No killer admits that he murdered his wife.

"If you go to the redtop rags with a scandal story I will put them out of business, and ensure you get no more clients. Do not mess with me, Russell. I have the law on my side."

"Silly me, I thought the law belonged to the people."

"Make it fast."

"So you do understand the law? Tell you what, let's cut a deal. You tell me about that night and I won't tell tales to the cops. I can't talk for you, but I'm a man of my word. Deal?"

He had rehearsed the alibi. It matched Lanigan's alibi point for point. They had been both reading from the same script. He had been drunk on that night. His friends had deposit him at a taxi-rank before eight in the evening. He recalled that he'd arrived home after nine to an empty house. I suspected he had drawn up the script. As long as the three of them stuck to it, he was safe. Having met Lanigan, I knew he'd stick to the script.

"How do you remember what time you arrived home?"

"What?"

"According to the alibi you were drunk. When I'm drunk I fall asleep and remember nothing. Did they teach you to remember the time when you're drunk whilst at law school?"

"This isn't about the will, is it? Who hired you?"

"The woman you murdered."

*

It was time to call it a day. It was time for a beer and a hot shower. Then I realised too late that I was in the middle of the traffic rush hour. People were going home from work, all in the same direction as me. The traffic snailed to a halt. I found an alley and parked the car.

I supped a beer and switched off. It's a good trait, the ability to switch off. Lots of men bring their work home with them and that defeats the whole purpose. Problems are best solved with a refreshed mind. Sure, I was certain Murphy had murdered his wife; but that's as far as I got. I didn't think about the corpse. I didn't think how a dead person could walk. I didn't think how a dead person could drink coffee. I just sat there in the pub and stared out the window.

As I've said, Dublin is a low-rise city. There are a couple of high-rise buildings, no more. Plans for the city with skyscrapers are nearly always shot down. The Irish don't like skyscrapers. It has to do with their history. They hate anyone looking down on them.

I phoned Jane. She was on her way home on the bus. There had been no phone calls to the office. She was all excited, and could not help blabbing her mouth off, even on a bus full of people. She told me about a date with her new boyfriend. She changed them more often than I changed my underpants. I never interfered in her love life. I was not trained in psychiatry.

"Darren Pringle is his name," she remarked.

"What did you say?"

"Why the sudden interest in my boyfriends, Jack? You weren't interested before in my love life. For your information, he's famous. He does be on the papers most weeks. He was on the paper last Sunday too."

"I told you to investigate him, not date him."

"Who knows how love works, Jack?"

"What is he? A nuclear scientist?"

"Is that your attempt at sarcasm, Jack? Didn't we talk about him, you and me? Let me refresh your memory because I think you're going senile. He is a style guru and a genius. He creates new fashions. He's going to change my clothes. He wants to make me look more mature."

I didn't even try to figure that out.

"You're letting a man older than your grandfather undress you? There's a name for that. I think it's called paedophilia. Are you serious?"

"Why do you always look for dirty meanings, Jack? That's what his job is. I'm fed up wearing old clothes. It must be six months since I had a new outfit. By the way, I'm running late already. Goodnight."

My phone went dead.

Jane spent more on clothes than an average working mother spent on her kids. I couldn't figure it out, not on what I paid her. Fashion stores were her favourite places in the whole world. I guess everybody has that favourite place in the world where they want to be. For Jane, it was the fashion store.

I lived in an apartment on the south side in Camden Street, over a shop. It was very convenient. If I forgot a carton of milk, I could slip out anytime and get it. The apartment had two bedrooms, a small kitchen, and a living room. I had a beer and sat down to watch the nine o'clock news. That's when the doorbell rang.

The clothes were the same, and her complexion. I invited her inside. She asked me to turn off the light. I promised to bring darkness after I made her coffee. As the kettle boiled, I watched her through the door opening. Then I snapped her picture on the phone when she wasn't looking. She didn't see me do it. I handed her the mug and switched off the light.

"What did he do with the murder weapon?"

"Dumped it, no doubt."

"Where'd he get it?"

"He had it in the house. It belonged to his grandfather who had fought in Germany. He was in the British Army. It was a war trophy. A Mauser, I think."

"Was it reported to the cops?"

"I don't think so."

"I met your best friend, by the way. Sarah Corbally. She warned you about marrying him? But you went ahead and married him anyway. She's pregnant now."

"I'm happy for her."

Yellow street lights filtered through the blinds. I tried to move closer, just to touch her. Maybe I was trying to prove to myself that she was real, not a figment of my imagination. There comes a time in every man's life when he begins to doubt his sanity. The man who doesn't question his own sanity is usually insane. It's one of those peculiar enigmas of human nature that nobody can explain. It was my time to question my sanity, to prove I wasn't insane.

However, she moved away.

"What are you doing, Jack?"

"Think I'm making a play for a corpse?"

"You're a man."

"Sure, but I'm not into necrophilia."

"So, you did go to school. I am impressed."

"I can tie my own shoelaces by myself too."

I gave her a rundown on progress so far. Her face twisted when I mentioned the visit to her husband – her former husband, that is. Somehow, she had found out where I lived. It wasn't something I advertised. She finished the coffee and I took the mug to the kitchen. When I returned, she wasn't on the sofa. She was gone, and I hadn't heard her leave.

CHAPTER FOUR

Another week began, and no change in the weather, or the horses.

I made a call to Charlie Bastable. He worked as a reporter on *The Tribune*. Charlie and I were old friends. He had a good nose for a story, especially if it stank. A lot of stories in Dublin stank more than a beached whale six months dead, but Charlie had to tread carefully because of the country's crazy libel laws. They were framed to protect the rich and powerful, and to punish the poor and the press.

He suggested meeting in a bar, but it was too early in the day for me. We met in a burger joint on Grafton Street. It was a bad time to meet because the place was filled with screaming kids and their parents. We were the same age, but Charlie looked much older. He had that hangdog look, as if he had the troubles of the world on his bony shoulders. I bought a couple of burgers and milkshakes. I knew that Charlie was out of his depth there. He'd have preferred a bar having a whiskey and a pint.

"How's biz, Charlie?"

"Terrible."

Charlie was much the same as an active dog sitting on a thistle. He wasn't happy unless he had something to bark about. That's just the way he was. Some men are happy all the time, some unhappy all the time. Charlie was one of the latter. Optimism or a brave new world was not part of his character.

"Why don't you write good news for a change?"

"Society at large expects bad news in a newspaper, Jack. If we printed good news we'd go out of business in a week. It's hard to have a happy face when you have to pen bad news every day. You've got to watch your back too, with all the libel lawyers in this corrupt city. What about you?"

"Have you heard of Paul Murphy?"

"I heard," Charlie muttered, eating his burger. "The cops are trying to frame him for the murder of his wife."

He had a habit of speaking with his mouth full. Well, we all have our faults. Me, I love the jumps. National hunt racing is the best sport in the world. I like a smoke as well, even if non-smokers treat me like a leper.

"I'm working on that case."

"You didn't tell me you were promoted to murder."

"It's long story. You don't think the husband killed her?"

"I know he didn't. You're knocking that thick head off a brick wall, Jack. The killer is even more important than the husband. He is as rich as Murphy, he has more clout than Murphy, and he has more contacts than Murphy. Furthermore, he is a politician.

They don't jail such important people like that in this fucken Mickey Mouse democracy. You think this is America?"

"Who are we talking about, Charlie?"

"Patience, Jack, I'm eating."

"It's about the will. You remember the case?"

Charlie wolfed down the food. I suspected he would not be formally invited to tea in Buckingham Palace. Crumbs clung to his lips like limpets. Charlie didn't wipe them off. He'd let the laws of gravity do that for him.

"Come clean, you're working on the murder, Jack."

"Okay. Can you tell me anything?"

"Attended the autopsy, didn't I? Murder by person or persons unknown. The coroner should be writing gags for comedians. Every dog on the street knows who killed her. Why not go out and ask them? Barry Allen murdered her. Sorry, let me rephrase that. Politicians don't do their own murdering, they get somebody else to do it for them. My editor wouldn't let me express an opinion in the newspaper for fear of litigation from his multiple army of lawyers."

"Allen? The former Minister for Finance?"

"That's who she worked for, didn't she? The same man who lorded over the Celtic Tiger. The same man who wrecked the economy. But unlike a functioning democracy where he'd been serving jail for ruining the country and taking bribes, he's out there writing books and planning a comeback. And guess what, Jack? The fools will vote him in again."

"Why should Allen have her killed?"

"Because she knew too much, dummy."

Charlie noisily slurped his milkshake through a plastic straw. It wasn't his fault. Charlie preferred whiskey, and they don't serve whiskey with a straw. It didn't bother me too much. After all, it was a cheap burger joint, not Buckingham Palace. There was no queen in the burger joint to insult. His bad table manners weren't noticed there.

"Enough to have her murdered?"

"He was blackmailing builders for kickbacks. He was taking bribes. He was a regular visitor to tax havens. He was cheating on his wife. A man who cheats on his wife will cheat on his country. And that's what we know about. What don't we know about him?"

"Think they were having an affair?"

"Possibly. Some women are drawn to power like a moth is drawn to a flame, usually with the same result."

"It depends on the woman, Charlie."

"Did you know the cops haven't even questioned him about the murder? Well, what do you expect when the politicians appoint the top brass in the cops? Political appointments have no place in a democracy. I've been writing that for years, but nobody takes a blind bit of notice. I feel like Cassandra sometimes."

"The horse?"

"Is that supposed to be a joke, or don't you know?"

"Did you happen to read the autopsy?"

"The State pathologist put her death around seven that night, with a margin of error thirty minutes each way. No doubt Allen has an alibi. He didn't pull the trigger himself, but he did give the orders."

"Do you have the name of the taxi driver who took the husband home that night?"

"Mickey Flanagan, works the rank near Trinity College. Don't let him charge you too much. I'm not talking about the fare either. Eh, care for a quick one?"

"Some other time, Charlie."

From the burger bar I took a tram out to see Sarah Corbally.

She was wearing the same dirty smock and painting a door. Her bump had grown a bit. I hadn't time for tea, and showed her the picture on the phone. Her head nodded up and down.

"Where did you get this?"

"Is that her?"

She studied the picture in silence. "Yes, that's Colleen. She is slightly paler, but there can be no doubt. Where did you get it? I have never seen her that pale before. She's ashen."

I avoided the question. What could I have told her? That her best friend was alive? That she had dropped in for tea after the coroner had pronounced her dead? That she had defied the laws of life and death?

"Did you attend the funeral?"

"Yes, she was cremated."

"What can you tell me about Barry Allen?"

"He is a liar and a cheat, but that's his profession. She did work for him, but she was not involved with him. I think she knew his character. Besides, he was married when she worked for him. His separation came afterwards."

"What about the funeral?"

"The cremation was very informal and much shorter than a burial. A few words were said, and her coffin vanished behind a screen. That was that. I can't say if that was her wish. After all, we were young and the subject never came up. The young don't think of death, do they?"

There could be no argument with that question. The facade of the Long Bar didn't welcome strangers with open arms, and I hadn't been there before. Nobody in uniform drank there. The characters who did hated the city, and its officials. It was a bar in a rundown district of the city near Sheriff Street. The irony tended to go unnoticed by the clientele. It was a place that regarded strangers as enemies. Every deadbeat druggie and his companions went there. They played pool and drank beer by the neck. Not hygienic, but good for the hardman image they saw in American gangster movies.

The whiff of marijuana filled the air with a fog of heady incense. Franky Mangan visited the place every day. I needed someone streetwise with an ear to the ground. That's why I went there on Sunday morning. Needless to say, I was greeted like the prodigal son with the killing of a fatted calf.

The blaring music suddenly stopped playing when I walked in. The tattooed headbangers at the pool table stood upright and glared at me. All the bar needed was a sign saying strangers might be expected to leave in a box. In a corner an addict is shot up. He wasn't too worried about hygiene either. The needle looked like it had been down a coal pit. There was a pantyhose between his teeth with one leg wrapped around his arm. At least I think it was an arm, although it might have been the branch of a dead tree. A short spurt of watery blood hit the wall like a drunk urinating in an alley.

I plucked up the courage to ask the barman if Franky was around. He was a body freak with no noticeable neck, and his head sat on his torso like a gigantic melon. He sported more steroid muscles than a convention of Mister Worlds. It didn't take a genius to figure out he pumped iron when not serving beer by the neck.

"Who wants to know?"

"That's my business."

"You're very tough for a small man."

"I don't wear my muscles on the outside."

As the stand-off continued in silence, who should stroll in but Franky Mangan. He spotted me and pointed to a corner table. A million names were carved on its wooden top. We sat down and I bought him a whiskey. He had a big sticking plaster on his nose. Franky was one of those characters who couldn't avoid accidents. He'd find a tree in the Sahara Desert to fall over.

"Ever hear of Paul Murphy, Franky?"

Franky was fifty and had been wearing the same

suit for more than fourteen years. His shirt had been white in the past, but that was a long time ago. He didn't care much for his appearance. The clothes matched his lifestyle because he lived from hand to mouth. But he did know what went down in the city, and that's why I was there on Sunday morning.

"I do, Jack. Murdered his mott. Why?"

"I'm on the case."

"So are the pigs. They won't get him."

"It's about the will, you know how it is."

"Where there's a will, there is relations. They tell me he has a new mott now. They say she has class. I don't know her name, but he had her up at the Lord Mayor's mansion in Dawson Street last week. Don't you read the gossip pages, Jack?"

Franky smiled at the little joke. He didn't read the gossip pages either. He got all the news on the street. Franky read the pages of runners in the betting shops. That's where we'd met.

"I'll look it up, Franky."

"Heard she can speak at least five different languages. I have enough trouble with English to last me a lifetime."

Franky had the look of a permanent drinker. He was skinnier than a whippet, and his face was lined. He lived for the next drink. That was his only worry, how to get the price of the next drink, and the next bet on the horses. He supplemented his simple lifestyle by robbery. Franky was a very good thief, and he was not violent. He was what they call a good thief, if that is not a contradiction.

"You get the news on the streets, Franky. Anyone you think I can contact about his wife's murder?"

Franky glanced around the place. It wasn't hard to figure out what he was thinking. He didn't want to be seen as a grass. He was expected to keep his lips buttoned up, just like the rest of them in the joint. They didn't volunteer information to the cops or to private eyes. As a matter of fact, they hated private eyes more than they hated cops. The cops chased bad guys because they had to, but private eyes did it for the money.

"Well," I said, standing up, "see you around."

I went outside and turned into an alley. Light snow was starting to fall, drifting on the city in soft flakes. After a few minutes, Franky joined me. I pulled out a packet of cigarettes and offered him one. He lit up the cigarette and dragged on it a couple of times. He rubbed his bloodless hands for warmth. Pulling up his collar, he gave me the word on the street.

"Maybe Calamity Casey can help, Jack," he puffed.

"Who?"

"Calamity Casey, former girlfriend of James Murphy, who just happened to be a brother of the murderer. Well, nobody can choose who he has for a brother. Chalk and cheese, the both of them."

"Why is she called Calamity?"

"Because anyone who dates her ends up dead. That's what happened to James Murphy. He ended up dead. Motts like that are just plain unlucky. I think it's in their genes."

"Where do I find her?"

"She lives out there in the sticks in at Inchicore, and they eat their young in that place. You'd want your head examined to go into some estates there. The pigs are issued with suits of armour when they patrol Inchicore. What day was that woman killed?"

"Christmas Eve last."

"Last Christmas, right?" He dragged on the cigarette like a man grasping for a lifebelt in a stormy sea. "Let me see, yeh, I seen the two of them together that night. Yeh. She was with Paul Murphy comin' out of a hotel down in Wexford Street. It was about four in the day."

"You sure, Franky? Murphy and Calamity Casey?"

"Yeh, I'm sure. They reckon she's from Conamara and they live on their wits over there since the famine. Shake hands with one of them and your fingers are robbed. She has red hair and green eyes. Some say dyed. I'm talking about the hair, not the eyes."

CHAPTER FIVE

Dusk was falling gently on the city when I drove down the quays to Inchicore. I felt braver than a wildebeest in a pride of lions. She must have been expecting an atomic attack because she lived in a concrete bunker of flats about four storeys high, with no visible windows. I parked the car under a lamp to deter thieves and continued the journey on foot. This part of the city was in darkness. The lights were broken, and pieces of glass littered the streets. You didn't have to be a genius to figure out why the block of flats had no windows. Nothing stirred except a slight breeze with a hint of the north.

Then I spotted movement in the dusk, and I heard the tap-tapping of a walking stick. It was Professor Alan Jones out for his nightly stroll. This old gent was known and disrespected in some parts of the city because of his views on poverty. He wanted to abolish it from the city. The fact that his message always fell on deaf ears didn't deter him from speaking out. The truth has a way of offending the powerful. He had unruly grey hair and wore thickset glasses. He dressed in a tweed coat and scarf, and he walked with the aid of a stick.

"Jack, you're off the beaten track."

"Hello, Professor."

"What are you doing in this neck of the woods?"

"On a case. Do you happen to know Calamity Casey?"

"I prefer calling her Mary Casey."

His walking stick rose up and pointed to the concrete bunker.

"Third floor, number thirty-six." He hesitated for a couple of seconds before continuing. "Know something, Jack, government ministers want to figure out why the poor hate the State. They house human beings in places like that with little or no amenities and then expect respect in return. Meanwhile, they pour money and privilege over their cronies and friends like a shower of golden rain. No wonder these people take to crime."

"It's a democracy. The politicians were voted in."

"If a person from this estate robs a shop, he's sent to jail. If a banker in a suit robs a billion from his bank, he gets to play golf in Florida. Just listen to the news and see if I'm wrong."

"The law states that all are equal in Dublin, Professor."

"What the law says and what the laws does are two opposite principles, Jack. You ought to know that. If we continue to treat some citizens as second-class citizens we are storing up trouble for ourselves in future. Mark my words."

The professor had a social conscience, but I was

trying to nail a killer. I thanked him and went inside the bunker. I had expected the lift to be broken, and it was. The stairway was concrete and dark, and the scent of urine was overpowering. A box of matches later, I reached the third floor. There was no response when I knocked on number thirty-six. I heard movement from inside, but the door wasn't opened.

"I need to talk to you, Mary. Hear me out, I'm not the law. I'm a private detective. The relatives of Colleen Murphy hired me. It's about her will. I'll pay for any information."

Slowly the door opened. It must have had a dozen locks.

I showed her an ID card through the small opening. Then I heard her open the locks. Her flat was no bigger than a shoebox, but it was clean and tidy. There was really nothing spectacular to see in Mary Casey, apart from the red hair and the green eyes. She was very pretty in an anaemic sort of way. I put her age at twenty, maybe a couple of years older. I asked her about Paul Murphy.

She denied ever knowing him. Of course, she was lying.

"You were seen coming out of a hotel with him on the day of the murder. I have it from someone who never gave me a bum steer. Look, Mary, I'm like a priest in a confession box. It won't go any farther than my ears."

"Whoever told you is a dirty liar."

"I can check with the hotel."

"Go ahead, see if I care."

"What was your relationship with him? Had it something to do with the fact that you dated his brother James?"

"I had no relationship with either of them."

"Seems I'm wasting my time. See you around."

"Hey, what about payment for information?"

"You have to give it to be paid."

That's all I got out of her. I thanked her for the time and headed back into the city. My abiding impression of Mary Casey was not the red hair or the green eyes. It wasn't the lies either. She was afraid of something out there, or someone. Let me rephrase that, she was terrified of someone out there.

Early next morning I drove down to Wellington Quay. I hung around sipping coffee in a nearby café and watching out for Philip Grogan. We'd met before briefly across a courtroom. I was gambling he wouldn't remember me because I wasn't important enough to be remembered. He'd sued the owners of a factory on behalf of his client who had broken into the factory to rob its contents. His client had fallen through the roof and sued the owner. His client had sustained no injuries, but that hadn't stopped the lawsuit. Grogan's client appeared in public using a pair of crutches. I can't say if the lawyer advised his client to use the crutches, but they were more likely to sway a jury than a man walking unassisted into the courtroom.

The insurance company had hired me to expose the scam. I'd taken pictures of the client playing hurling at weekends. That's a game not usually played with crutches. It's usually played with hurleys and is extremely physical. His crippled client had sprinted up and down the field faster than a hare. When presented with the evidence in court, Grogan had denied all knowledge. His client had appeared to be genuinely injured, otherwise he would never have taken on the case.

I saw him ascending the steps carrying a briefcase and wearing a fawn crombie coat. He had a lean build, slightly balding on top. I followed him up the steps. Before the receptionist could tell me he was in court, I told her to mention Happy Days. She picked up the phone and the door opened. That password was getting me into lots of places that didn't want to meet me. My gamble paid off. He showed no signs of recognition. He had a lot of impressive law books stacked on shelves. There was no desk in the room, only leather chairs. They were more intimate. They gave the impression that he was a friend to all injured parties ground down by the system. He was a champion of the working man against the same system that had made him rich.

"Happy Days?"

"Yes, where you spent Christmas Eve with your friends. I bet you didn't tell that to the cops, never mind your wife. Let's cut the denials. I have proof you were there. You're in the business. You should know that proof is king."

"What proof?"

"Enough to put a serious dent in your income."

"I do not deny it, but it was on official business."

"Christmas Eve is a busy time in your profession? I checked a dozen law firms. Not one opened on that day." He was on the point of denial, so I played it tough. "Most of the buxom girls who work in these places are illegal immigrants. Some of them were trafficked here for sex. They'll talk if the cops threaten them with deportation. Believe me, they'll sing louder than song thrush after a mate."

He was in a corner. I knew it and he knew it. So he started to talk. He said that the owner of the club, Madame Wu, preferred to do her business at the club. That's why he had gone there on Christmas Eve. He had not engaged in any sexual activities. He had read a book instead. I didn't enquire about the title.

"That's not what I heard."

"It's the truth nonetheless."

Of course, he was lying. It went with the territory. Two could play the lying game, and I did. My case was much stronger than his. He was protecting a murderer, and I was trying to nail him I upped the stakes with more lies.

"One of the girls who works there is my client. She told me you participated in an orgy. She is prepared to tell that story in court if necessary, that's if she's threatened with deportation. Can you afford to have that sort of thing come up in court? Your reputation would be holed below the water line. As for your marriage…"

He looked at me and I looked back. He was playing for high stakes, but I had nothing to lose. I had upped the ante, so to speak.

He couldn't see the bet because he was holding a nothing hand.

He had to talk next. I could afford to be dumb until the cows came home. This was not a courtroom where he held most of the aces.

"We were there, three of us. There was Paul, David, and myself. We had a bottle of champagne. Paul and David... well, they availed of the services on hand. I did not. I am a happily married man."

"So is the pope."

He pretended not to hear the comment.

"We left the premises at six. I remember the time because I had to call home. We went for a few drinks in Temple Bar. At fifteen minutes to eight we looked for a taxi. At eight we put Paul in a taxi. He was very drunk. Certainly too drunk to have killed his wife. Besides, he could not have killed her. He was with us at the time."

The same alibi, the same times, the same lies. They had rehearsed it down to a fine art. Murphy was safe so long as they all kept to the script. But it was only as strong as the weakest link. The cops should have been putting more pressure on him because he was that weak link.

*

Mickey Flanagan worked the taxi rank near Trinity College. Another driver pointed him out. He was in his fifties and should have been a brain surgeon. At least, that's the impression he gave me. He was cut out for better things than driving a taxi. My card made no impression, but a twenty grabbed his attention. Christmas Eve is the busiest night in the year for taxi drivers. He shouldn't have recalled all the details of the fare, but he did.

"I picked him up at eight on the dot. He was very drunk, but he was a proper gentleman. The traffic was heavy that night. Normally the time is forty minutes, but it took me an hour or more to get him home. We reached the house about ten minutes past nine."

"That what you told the cops?"

"Why not? It's the truth."

"How'd he pay? Credit card?"

"Cash. I don't do cards."

"You drive him to his front door?"

"I did that."

"Any car parked outside?"

"The lights were on in the house, but I saw no car."

"See anyone near the house?"

"I did not."

"Did he use a mobile phone in the taxi?"

He hadn't been prepared for that question. Whoever had told him what to say hadn't thought of that. He had to think long and hard. He would not have cut it as a brain surgeon. But I didn't want to spoil his day by telling him that.

"Why should he use a phone in my cab?"

"To tell his wife he'd be late for supper. To tell her he was on the way. They were supposed to have dinner at seven, and he didn't get into your cab until an hour later. According to your story, it was after nine when you left him home. That means he was two hours late for dinner. Women tend to get very upset looking across a table for two when the second person isn't there. It ruins the conversation."

"I don't remember."

"Funny that, you remember everything else. Do you recall if he had a mobile phone with him?"

"There's a fare, I have to go."

He didn't have it on the night of the murder. Phone records would have placed him near the scene at the time his wife was murdered. Only a fool brings his phone when he kills his wife.

Paul Murphy was a lot of things, but he was no fool.

The nice waitress in the Internet café found the piece about Paul Murphy meeting the Lord Mayor. Amy Reddy wore a skirt and blouse, with a necklace. She was beautiful in the exaggerated way of women who hang around rich men. Murphy had his hand on her waist, in a protective fashion. I needed to find out where she lived. I left a message in the bookie shop for Franky Mangan to phone, and the price of the call.

Thursday morning, and I was eating a bun and drinking tea in the office when the phone rang. Jane said it was Charlie Bastable. He invited me out to lunch, but I preferred solid food to the lunches he drank. His lunches tended to last all day.

"Some information might be of use, Jack. The brother of Paul Murphy was running around with a woman called Calamity Casey. They were eco-warriors, holing up in buildings and stopping motorways being built. The family wasn't too pleased with all the bad publicity. After all, Paul is a prominent member of the legal profession, and here was his brother getting arrested every week. A year ago, James Murphy was killed in a car crash. He was driving a sports car at the time."

"What are you saying, Charlie?"

"I thought you understood English. Want me to spell it out for you? He was an eco-warrior. He wore his lair long and braided like Bob Marley. That sort don't drive cars. They prefer driving covered wagons. What was he doing driving a car? A Ferrari sports car at that?"

I switched on the TV to catch the 2:30 at Leopardstown. Jane came in and told me to switch over to the news. It was urgent. Superintendent William Kenny appeared on screen. He was not my favourite person. I'd worked with him in the past, and that time had not created any happy memories. Now he was hogging the limelight in a crisp blue uniform before a forest of microphones.

He was a glutton for publicity, believing daily exposure could compensate for an inability to do his job. Kenny was after the Commissioner's job, and would do whatever it took. The fact that he was a civil servant first and a cop second would not be allowed to get in his way.

"A breakthrough?" a reporter asked.

"We are following a line of inquiry. Of course we cannot name the suspect for legal reasons. It's only a matter of time before we have enough evidence to pick up the suspect."

"Is it a man or a woman?"

"That's all for now. Thank you."

I picked up the phone and called Dermot Brady on his mobile.

He was also a cop, but unlike Kenny he was not political. He believed a cop should concentrate on putting criminals behind bars, and not stabbing colleagues in the back to get promoted. I asked him about the conference that Kenny had called.

"There is no breakthrough, Jack. The case has gone cold. It was Kenny's idea to call the conference. He thought it would throw a scare into the killer. What's your interest in this?"

"His wife hired me to catch the killer."

"His wife? Are you crazy? She's dead."

"I'll fill you in when we meet."

CHAPTER SIX

Jane listened with an impassive face, looking at her reflection in a mirror. She's had her hair changed again. The flagrant pink has been replaced with a subtle shade of black. It was more orderly too. Obviously she had been taking advice from her new boyfriend, the guru of fashion.

"The hairdo suits you."

"Darren does have great taste."

"I hope you haven't discussed the case with him."

"What case is that, Jack? Would it be the dead woman who wants you to put her husband behind bars? Or the invisible woman who somehow came here and left without me seeing her? He'd drive me to the nearest funny farm if I told him that."

"She hasn't rang?"

"Jaysus, Jack, you need help."

Amy Reddy lived in the Smithfield area of the city near the tram line. Franky had told me she drove a blue BMW. I took the tram and walked across the cobblestones to the complex at the corner. A cold wind swept across the square and I pulled up the collar of my coat. As I passed an alley a pair of large hands seized me and slammed me up against a wall. He had the features of a boxer who's been in too many fights. I really don't wish to get personal when talking about a fellow human being, but he was the ugliest man you ever did see. He had a couple of broken teeth, and his breath didn't smell of honey and roses. No agency would have hired him to advertise toothpaste.

"Amy Reddy don't like to be disturbed," he warned.

He was too strong for a normal human being. He had to be tanked up on crack cocaine. His eyes were all over the place, rolling like a Las Vegas slot machine. They were finding it hard to keep in focus. But they always returned to me.

"I don't know what you're talking about."

The worst mistake any man can make is threaten a private eye, especially one with a name like Jack Russell. I made a grab for his throat and we began to fight. I'm pretty good in a fight and can punch way above my weight. His head rolled back a few times when my head connected. He should have gone down in pain, but he didn't. I hit him everywhere with everything, and still he beat me hands down. He was bigger and stronger, and he was a better scrapper. We both acknowledged that straight fact. He left me there lying in the rain bloodied and bruised. I was waiting for the boot to come in, but he must have been too tired for that. It could not have been an act of mercy to spare the boot.

Just when I thought every god was against me, a blue BMW rolled up. I expected it to roll past. Nobody stopped to help, not in the modern city.

They simply stepped over you to get to where they were going, or stooped down to rob you. I recognised Amy Reddy emerging from the car.

"Can I be of help?"

"Only if you're a surgeon from a war zone."

"Should I drive you to a hospital?"

"No, it's just my ego that's broken."

She smelled of lavender and Provence, a place I've always meant to visit. Her arm helped me to my feet. I was sorer than a bear's head, but no broken bones. A concierge at the door of the complex helped me to the lift. She lived on the top floor. The whiskey she gave me dulled the pain, but not the humiliation. My pride hurt worse than my body.

"A mugging, was it?"

She wore her blonde hair long, shaping her face. She had good taste in clothes too. Her outfit was simple but classy. The blouse was white and the skirt black. I said a friend of hers had beaten me up, and described him. She denied any knowledge of him, and his description didn't ring a bell. Or so she said.

"Probably stoned out of his head."

"Yet he knew my name. How?"

"Why ask me?"

"Maybe he was hired by Paul Murphy to protect you."

"I don't see why. He's not my fiancé."

"Maybe he wants to be."

"Maybe I don't want what he wants."

"The rich usually get what they want in this country."

"Do you believe everyone has a price?"

"That's been my experience."

"You are obviously moving in the wrong circles."

"I can't afford to move in higher circles."

"It's not a question of money."

"Good, I can't join then."

"Try working harder."

She had an answer for everything. The apartment was modern and furnished in muted colours. I went to the bathroom to clean up. There were no signs of a man in the bathroom, no toothpaste tube squeezed in the middle, no dirty socks thrown on the tiled floor. She lived alone. My face was the same colour and texture as a butcher's block. The hot water cleared it up a bit.

I had come to ask her questions, but now they were the last thing on my mind. I was easy in her company. There were no pregnant pauses or lapses in conversation. We drank whiskey and we watched the gas flames light up the room. She didn't ask any personal questions, so I didn't have to answer any. I forgot, too, about the difference in our ages. I was at least a dozen years older, and not nearly as pretty. It didn't cross my mind that she could have been setting me up, not until later when I was alone.

"What sports do you like?"

"National hunt, you know, jumping over fences."

"Isn't that cruel on horses?"

"It's more cruel on the punters who back them."

"Ah, so you're a gambler."

"One of my vices. I'm a private investigator the rest of the time. Before you ask, the pay is lousy and the hours long. The perks can be seen on my face. So I'm no husband material."

"Then why do it?"

"I tried nuclear fission, but it didn't work out."

"Did you step on somebody's toes?"

"The beating? It comes with the territory."

"Whose territory?"

"Have you a jealous husband hidden in the closet?"

"No," she said, showing her left hand.

I showed her mine, and she laughed. It was a spontaneous laugh. My knuckles were bruised and bloody. Comparing my hand with hers was the same as comparing a gorilla to the Mona Lisa.

"Well, I lost the fight. What do you do?"

"Computer software. Have you heard of computers?"

"Sure, they figure out the odds for horse races."

"That's one way of putting it. Do you live nearby?"

"I would if I could afford the rent."

"Are you investigating me by any chance?"

So I gave her the story about the will. I didn't want her to think I was a crazy man, so I never mentioned the corpse. Not once. She listened and looked at me with those eyes. She offered me another drink and I didn't say no.

"What can you tell me about Paul Murphy?"

"We sit on the same charity board. I know people believe he murdered his wife, but I believe a man is innocent until proven guilty in a court of law. What do you believe?"

"Murphy? He murdered his wife."

"Well, at least you're forthright."

"You're safe, as long as you don't marry him."

I hadn't noticed the passage of time, until a clock somewhere struck twelve times. Only when I tried to get up did I remember the beating. My ribs ached and my jaw ached. She helped me to my feet, and I smelled that lavender again. I dreamt of Provence for a moment or two. However, flights to Spain were cheaper, and so was the wine.

"Have you a name?"

"Jack Russell, and no cracks."

"Presumably you know mine, since you were investigating me. It's Amy Reddy, just in case you got the wrong woman."

"I got the right woman."

"You can stay the night."

"I never sleep with a girl on a first date."

"Old-fashioned too. I wasn't trying to seduce you."

"I wasn't refusing."

"In there," she said, pointing to a spare bedroom. "The door has a lock in case you feel threatened."

The offer was too good to take up. She called a taxi and gave her address. I knew it would be there in minutes. That's how it is with taxis. When you're in a hurry, they're never on time. This one was waiting downstairs.

Next day Jane went out and came back with a bag of plasters and bandages. My ribs resembled the rainbow, except rainbows don't have black. She gave out as she worked, and I didn't listen. I was thinking of Amy Reddy and those eyes. Then I remembered that I had forgotten to give her my phone number.

"What's up with you, Jack? You have the look of puppy at a birthday party. Don't tell me you're in love. God help the poor girl is all I can say. An old fool is the worst fool."

"Less lip, Jane, and more bandages."

"The corpse, is it?" she said, giggling.

"I'm going to question your boyfriend soon."

"Jack, I warn you, if you break it up I'll never talk to you again as long as I live. Never. I'll get a job somewhere else."

"Is that a promise?"

The phone rang and she picked it up. "Call later, can't you see I'm busy?" she said. "God, why can't they pick a better time to ring, and me with my hands full?"

"Who was that, Jane?"

"Some woman. Hold still. Typical bachelor. What you need is a wife. Problem is, most women have good taste."

"What woman?"

"She'll call back if it's urgent."

I took a day off to recover my fragile ego, and pigged out on beer and burgers. That night I watched an old movie. The heroine reminded me of Amy. When the doorbell rang once, I thought it was her. I hadn't given her my address, but I reckoned she could find me if she wanted. My hands hurt and I had difficulty opening the door. She wasn't Amy.

She was standing at the door with a couple of long beers and two brown bags in her hands. The aroma told me the bags had fish and chips inside with lots of vinegar. I didn't recognise Anne Neary at first because she was smiling. Also, she wasn't wearing glasses or dowdy clothes. She was dressed for going out on the town, not sitting at a desk. She wore her hair loose, and her dress tight. It was a lethal combination.

"What happened to you?"

"I fell down a stairs."

"Pushed, more likely," she smiled.

Beware the woman who smiles when she's after something.

She took in my tiny apartment in a single glance. Anne had no problem finding the kitchen. It was too small to miss. Meanwhile I went to the bathroom and checked up on my face. There was a cut above my right eye and heavy bruising on my chin. The hot water hurt worse than an angry jellyfish. I returned to the living room and sat down. She found a bottle opener and gave me a beer by the neck.

"Vinegar or not?"

"Vinegar."

"I bought one of each, just to be sure."

So we ate the fish and chips with our fingers and sipped the beer with our lips. She was after something, and I suspected it wasn't my body. There was a lot of silence going down. I waited for her next move.

"Listen, Jack, we got off on the wrong foot. I just came here to say sorry. Please accept my apology. I was having a bad day."

"Apology accepted."

"That's what I love about you. Some men just hold a grudge. Us girls don't hold a grudge, not at all. Don't get me wrong here, Jack. I'm not anti-male or anything, but they find it hard to forgive and forget. It's a man thing."

"I've forgotten already."

"The beating hasn't spoiled your good looks."

I hadn't been accused of that before. I resembled something found in an Egyptian tomb. A blanket of bandages was stretched around my ribcage, and my face was no oil painting. I had taken one hell of a beating. But I wasn't complaining. Every private eye takes a beating sooner or later. It goes with the territory. It could have been much worse. I was grateful he hadn't killed me.

"You still working on the deceased's will?"

"Last time I heard."

"Mr Murphy is willing to hand it over to you."

"Is that why you're here?"

She sipped the beer and eyed me up closely. I didn't have to work my brains hard trying to figure out why she was dressed in red. I knew it was for my benefit. Some women think a red dress turns a man on, like a bull. It depends what's inside the dress that turns a man on. If she'd been wearing white, it wouldn't have crossed my mind for a second. But she wasn't wearing white, she was wearing red. It didn't suit her. The dress wasn't right either. I could tell she was very uncomfortable. It just wasn't her style. She was self-conscious about the cleavage too.

"Colleen Murphy was mixed up in something bad. That's what I came here to tell you, Jack. She had a drug problem – cocaine. Paul supported her habit because he loved her. I think she was killed for a drug debt."

Colleen wasn't the cocaine type, at least not from what I'd heard about her. But this sort of thing often happened in a murder case. It's called muddying the waters. Throw out an accusation, and the cops have to follow it up. It wastes time, and it gives the killer a breathing space.

"Did she snort or inject?"

"Snorted it by the kilo. No puncture wounds."

She was feeding me a line, and I didn't know why. Either she was acting on her own, or somebody had coached her. So I listened and let her talk. The fish tasted real good. It was just the right shade of brown on the outside and the right shade of white on the inside. It was real cod too, not dogfish tarted up to taste like cod.

"Paul tell you where he was that day?"

"No, we have a strictly business relationship."

Next day I checked the record of the cremation at Glasnevin cemetery. The ashes had been placed in an urn and given to her husband. No evidence of foul play can be obtained from ashes.

Afterwards I drove out to her house in Killiney, near the sea. My mind wasn't on work. I could smell lavender in the car. I timed the journey, and it took forty minutes. My face had somewhat healed up, and I could smile now without hurting. My body was black and blue, but the bruises were out of sight. The day was cold with a hint of snow in the still air.

I drove along the cliff road to the house with the sea on my left and the gated houses of the rich and famous on my right. I was in Killiney, and the quality of the road proved that the rich and famous lived out there. The road where I lived could have doubled for the surface of the moon. I located the house behind wrought iron gates. It had turrets like a castle in Bavaria.

CHAPTER SEVEN

Maria Mendez came from Brazil to work in a beef plant in the West of Ireland some years back. There had been scare about mad cow disease and the plant closed. She came to Dublin and got a job as a cook for Paul Murphy and his wife. After the murder her employment was terminated. I eventually managed to locate her by phoning the dole offices. I gave the man on my number and asked him to give her my number.

She called on Tuesday, dole day. Her English wasn't good, but we managed to communicate. She hadn't been in the house on the day of the murder. Colleen had given her time off to spend with her family in Brazil. She'd flown to London to catch the plane to Rio a couple of days previously. She could tell me little except the tension between her former employers. It had been growing day by day.

I was driving down the quays to the office when I spotted a man in a grey duffel coat. He was pacing quickly in the direction of the office. Although the hood of the coat was raised against the cold, I recognised the peculiar walk. It was Detective Dermot Brady. I stopped the car and he jumped in.

"We need to talk, Jack. Drive."

So I drove out to Dollymount Strand through the crawling morning traffic. We could talk there. He said nothing on the way, just drumming fingers on the dashboard. He had a big hand for a man who could also think. The windblown strand was deserted apart from a woman and a dog. White waves crashed along the sand in rolls of sound.

"What are you mixed up in, Jack?"

"How long have we known each other? Twenty years since we were in the force together? Maybe I'm crazy, but let me tell you something about the Murphy murder case. Details were not released for operational reasons about the type of weapon used to kill her. What if I told you it was a German Mauser from World War Two?"

His expression told me all I needed to know. Slowly we walked along the beach and I told him everything. He was a friend, my best friend. He had always been there for me. He would tell me if I needed a psychiatrist. That's what a friend is for, to tell you something nobody else is prepared to tell you.

"I'll tell you another thing, Dermot. She wasn't killed in the car. She was killed elsewhere and driven up the mountains by her killer. If you find out who drove him back to the house, this case can be solved."

"You're telling me where she was killed, Jack?"

"In her kitchen."

"We had a forensic team go over that house, room by room. The kitchen was the most likely place because of the tiled floor. It's easier to clean tiles than carpets. We found nothing. A bullet is messy. It causes splatter on the ceiling, on the top of fridges where they can't be seen, everywhere. She was not killed in the house."

"She told me she was killed in her kitchen."

The woman with the dog came closer and we stopped talking.

We let her pass, watching the waves roll along the shore. They were louder than thunder. Perhaps they were trying to tell me I was crazy.

"A corpse told you she was killed in her kitchen. I hope you realise what you've just said?" He stopped to let the woman with the dog pass. It sniffed my leg before moving off. "What's she after, Jack? We both agree she can't be dead. The next step is to find out what she wants. What's her motive? What's driving her about this murder? Are you meeting her soon?"

"She contacts me… So I'm not mad, Dermot?"

"That's debateable. Next time she rings to make an appointment, call me. I'll tail her. There is an answer to every puzzle. All you need is the key to unlock the puzzle. Can you get her fingerprints? She might have a record."

"Right. Did the victim have brown hair and blue eyes?"

"Colleen Murphy? Yes. Why?"

"So has she. Her face is identical too."

"Get her fingerprints next time. Look, any good make-up artist can create an image. Or that sort of stuff can be accessed online. A word of warning, Kenny is in charge of this case. It's high profile. Solve this, and he gets the Commissioner's job. That's what he's after."

There was no need for further words or explanations. We both realised that Superintendent Kenny was a civil servant first and a cop second. Promotion was more important than keeping the public safe. He was after the top job and the salary that went with it, not to mention the Rolls Royce pension. He was after that job and would let nothing stand in his way.

"No gun was found, Dermot?"

"No, and it's my hunch it won't be either. Colleen Murphy had no family. I'm not talking about her husband, I'm talking about a real family. A family is the people who'll always take you back. A family can offer comfort in troubled times. I like to think I'm her family now, and I won't rest until I jail her killer."

"You believe Murphy killed her?"

"Who else? We know it, and he knows we know it, but proof is another matter. If we can break one of their alibis, the rest will throw Murphy to the wolves. At this time, though, they are sticking together like glue. We've had the three of them in and they all have the same alibi. That proves to me that the alibis were concocted to protect the killer."

"Put enough pressure on Grogan and he'll crack."

"He uses the law as a shield, but I'll keep on him."

"Where's her car?"

"We have it. Nothing showed up. We found her prints and none others. He wore gloves that night of course. But even if we'd found his prints, so what? She was his wife. A husband has been known to drive his wife's car."

"She was killed by a single bullet to the chest?"

"Yes," he said, hunkering down on the sand. He grabbed a handful and clenched it into a ball. Brady was a good cop, one with a conscience. He was very methodical, and never jumped to conclusion. He would never give up hunting the killer.

*

The woman who opened the door of the mansion in Rathgar didn't need a course of slimming pills. Rathgar used to be a genteel suburb of the city where nice people lived. Then the Celtic Tiger looped along and the new rich started to buy it up. If Rita Piggot had turned sideways she'd have been marked absent. I asked to see her husband, and Rita asked not too politely what for. She was told that I was willing to discuss that with her husband, not with her. That got her hair standing up like she'd seen a ghost.

"We have no secrets," she claimed.

"So how does it feel to be alone in the world?"

At that moment I realised who wore the pants in her marriage. It wasn't the one with the penis who wore them. Not that I believe the one with the penis should be the boss either. Marriage should be a two-way thing, a shared state, whether one partner has a penis or not.

"I rent an office from him down on City Quay. The toilet is out of order and it needs insulation. He's been promising to do something for the past year. Either it's fixed before Christmas, or I want a rent reduction. I'm talking fifty percent here."

She reacted as if I'd accused her of child murder.

"Fucken tenants are all the same, always complaining."

"Another thing, the law says receipts must be issued for rent payments. I pay in cash, but your husband always forgets to bring along the receipt book. He never forgets the day when the rent is due, however. Tell him to fix the problems, or I'll make a phone call to the Revenue."

"Is that a threat?"

"No, it's a promise."

In the late afternoon I had my head under the bonnet when the boxer who beat me up wheeled past. He didn't see me, but I saw him. He was riding a Norton motorcycle painted black with city plates. I'd been having trouble starting the car. The damp fog rolling in from the sea affected the glow plugs. I drove an old VW Golf 4-door that had seen better days, but it was more of a friend than a car. It was a good car to drive, except when the fog rolled in from the sea. It needed to be replaced, but that took money. That was in short supply since the downturn.

I left the car and hailed down a taxi. The motorbike was stuck in a traffic jam. The taxi driver followed him and complained about the state of the city and how hard it was to make a decent living. I told him he should try my line of business. The motorbike headed out of the city, taking the north road towards the airport. In the suburb of Drumcondra it wheeled left and stopped outside a red-bricked Victorian house, three storeys. He climbed the grey granite steps and rang the doorbell. The face of the man who opened the door was better known across the city than the face of Elvis.

Barry Allen, former Minister of Finance, was one of the principal architects of the Celtic Tiger, and its subsequent demise. He was the biggest player in the last government before it was kicked out of office by the electorate for putting the country up to its neck in hock to the International Monetary Fund. He liked to call himself Honest Barry. I bought the Barry, but not the Honest part. Anyone who feels the need to call himself honest is usually a crook.

Allen wore his greying hair tousled and his suit crumpled. But he could wear a black tuxedo with the best of them when the need arose. He gave lectures in his tuxedo on the success of the Celtic Tiger. He never gave lectures on its collapse.

I exited the taxi and climbed up the steep granite steps. This time the door was opened by a woman in a business suit. She could have been a mistress or an acolyte. When she denied Allen was at home I assumed she was training for politics.

"Tell him it's about the murder of Colleen Murphy," I said, passing over my card. "He's a civic-minded man. He'll talk to me. This is my phone number. I'm available 24/7."

The house had dormer windows, projecting from the wall. I could see inside. Two persons were seated on a leather sofa. One was Barry Allen. The second person was Amy Reddy. They were in deep conversation.

*

I was having bacon at home and sunnyside eggs when the phone rang. The clock said it was nearing midnight. I recognised the acolyte's voice. Mister Allen, she said, had agreed to meet me. I turned pink with happiness.

Allen sat in his constituency office in Drumcondra wearing the crumpled suit of his image. Nearby, a young woman sat at a computer console wearing his face. I presumed it was his daughter. I hung around reading a paper with people looking for favours. At noon Allen called me into his office.

"Hello," he beamed. "What's this your name is?"

"Russell."

"Of course I'm aware of that, Mr Russell. I know all your family too. The best family in the city. Not the slightest trouble with the law. That's what we need, honest citizens. It's your first name that I don't recall."

"It's Jack."

My hand was pumped and squeezed. That sort of thing tended to impress lots of voters. Sincerity. If you can fake that you've got it made. He could fake it better than any chameleon up a green tree.

He asked how he could help. I told him I was investigating the murder of Colleen Murphy. I told him she had an aunt in Australia who wasn't satisfied about the pace of the investigation.

I was playing poker again, but against a politician.

"I fail to see what this has to do with me."

"I tailed a scumbag who beat me up to your house yesterday. I watched him walk up the steps. I saw you open the door. Why did you have him beat me up?"

"You must be mistaken, Jack," he replied. "I have not seen or met any man of that description. In fact, I was not at home yesterday. I was out doing constituency work all day. Isn't that right, Caroline?"

"True," his daughter Caroline lied.

She was obviously contemplating a career in politics too, a chip off the old block. She would go far. Any person who could lie with a sincere face and tongue was sure to become party leader. Lying was most essential for that office.

"Maybe I need glasses."

"We all make mistakes, Jack."

"By the way, you promised to fix the road in Camden Street where I live. It's costing me a fortune in shock absorbers."

"It's the civil servants, Jack. They're a lazy shower. I told them a dozen times to get that road fixed. Now unfortunately I'm out of office. But when we're back in power I'll have it fixed."

He lied so convincingly that I almost believed him. He was hiding something, but I didn't know what or why. I threw a few more questions at him, but he avoided them. It took years of practice to evade questions that skilfully. It would need something more substantial to get him to talk.

Next morning I did the rounds, handing out pictures of Colleen Murphy to pubs and hotels. I was trying to find out if anybody had seen her on the day she was murdered. But that was a year back and people tend to forget as time passes. I drew blank after blank. Over soup and a sandwich, I phoned the garage and am met with a reply that they're having problems finding parts for the car.

"She's very old, Jack."

"Ten years is not that old for a VW."

"I'll phone you when she's ready."

I was having a bad day and it was not getting any better. The sofa in the corner of the hotel looked inviting, and I sat down to rest my feet. I must have nodded off for a minute or two because the phone in my pocket woke me up.

"What's the name of the corpse, Jack?" asked Jane.

"How many times…?"

"Don't blow a gasket. Some woman called Amy Reddy asked for your mobile number. Do I give it out? Don't tell me we have a second client. Oh, the pressure."

"Give it out."

"Would you like me to feed the world too, Jack?"

The phone rang, and I told Amy I was in Blooms Hotel down in Temple Bar. It was about noon when she arrived. She was dressed in a grey coat with a matching wide hat. She refused a sandwich, but agreed to a soup.

"You're a hard man to find, for a detective."

"I forgot to say thanks."

"Don't mention it. Why are you playing hard to get?"

"Me? I don't understand."

"You didn't call, you didn't write…"

She had heard the same monkey joke. We laughed at the same time. The day got much better. The sun came out of hiding and lit up the table where we sat. I forgot about seeing her with Allen. She had a smile that made bad things easy to forget.

"Do you have a tuxedo?"

"No, but I know a good rental shop."

There was a charity ball in the Gresham Hotel on December the twentieth. She had two tickets. It was for the people sleeping rough in Dublin. The Celtic Tiger had created lots of casualties. She reminded me that it didn't take war to create casualties. Most people had already forgotten that lesson.

After she left I continued making enquiries. Sooner or later I had to run into Charlie Bastable, and I did. He was having his usual lunch of Guinness washed down with a whiskey or three. Charlie got lots of stories in pubs, although he had to sort out the lies from the truth. I declined his offer of drink.

"I did a bit more digging, Jack. Remember we talked about James Murphy, the deceased brother of Paul?"

"Sure. He was running around with Calamity Casey."

"That poor girl is damaged, Jack. Did you ever read The Great Gatsby, by Fitzgerald? Best book ever to come out of America, no matter what the so-called experts say. There is a great line in that book. The narrator said that the rich are careless people. They damage others."

I didn't know what he was talking about. He

would explain it, but only after he downed the pint. Meanwhile, I handed out pictures of Colleen Murphy in the pub. More blanks, and I came back to Charlie.

"James and Calamity were an item, as they say nowadays. They were in love. His parents were, and are barristers. The first son followed them into the profession, but James rebelled. He and Calamity climbed trees to stop motorways. They squatted in vacant buildings earmarked for development..."

"Will this be finished before Christmas?"

"Patience, Jack. The family tried to bribe Calamity to stay away from James. Trying to bribe a woman in love! Then last Christmas Eve, Paul met her in a hotel, when he was supposed to be in that Chinese brothel. He offered to buy her a three-bedroom apartment if she'd stop asking questions."

"What time?"

"Ah, so now I have your attention. At four o'clock in the hotel, when he was supposed to be in that Chinese brothel. You see, some months before that meeting the family had bought James a sports car. They had also reminded him of his duties. So he'd dumped Calamity, and drove his sports car into a wall. Careless people."

Only now could I understand her bitterness. Colleen Murphy was dead, maybe she was lucky. Mary Casey was alive, but trapped in a hell not of her making. I reminded myself to read good literature in future, and not *The Racing Post*. Charlie had solved one puzzle, but I was no closer to nailing the killer.

"So Paul Murphy could not have killed his wife on the same day that he tried to bribe Calamity," Charlie continued. "I'm not talking time here, Jack, I'm talking about planning. The murder would have required a concentrated mind. It would have required planning that only a political mind could have conjured up, one without a conscience. No, Allen had her killed."

CHAPTER EIGHT

The VW was fixed and is ready to drive away. Big Val Donnegan wiped his hands on an oily rag, nodding his great head. He owned a small garage in a laneway at the rear of Rathmines Road. Val wore a blue garage overall and a peaked blue cap. The cap was advertising an oil company, but I doubt if he was getting paid for it. Val was not a celebrity after all. Big Val loved cars. He'd have worked on them for nothing, except he had a wife and kids to feed.

He could talk about them day and night, and he did. I felt sorry for his wife.

"I had to change the glow plugs, Jack."

"That same problem again?"

"Yeh. They weren't genuine parts."

"That so?"

"Yeh. Who fitted them?"

"You did, Val."

In the afternoon I drove back to the office, wondering why I hadn't heard from my employer. Then the fates intervened, and the phone rang. I was in traffic, but I took the call anyway. No number came up on my phone.

"Tonight," she said. "I'll call later."

Back at the office, I made a call to Dermot Brady. He was free that night, and ready to act. Jane was reading the gossip pages of a magazine. I told her not to pay the rent when it was due until we got a reduction. I doubted if she was listening.

"I see that Paul Murphy is engaged."

"What? Show me that."

"And you always slagging me off for reading this, Jack."

She was about twenty and a model with a good advertising cleavage and white teeth. They were in Paris, with the Eiffel Tower in the background. The same city of light where he'd married Colleen. Apparently the model didn't care about the rumours hanging over her future husband. In showbiz, there is no such thing as bad publicity.

"Speaking of old men and young girls, how is your love life going down with Pringle? Do I hear wedding bells?"

"I dumped him… well, he dumped me."

"Good, find someone your own age."

"Look who's giving advice."

"Tell me anything you can about Pringle."

"Colleen Murphy bought her clothes from him, and I mean the woman who was killed, not the figment of your imagination. He was with her on the morning she was killed. He measured her…"

"Measured her? Where? When?"

"Jaysus, Jack. Don't bite my head off. He measured her at his shop a month before Christmas. He delivered the dress to her around noon on Christmas Eve. She wanted it to be a surprise for her husband. They were having a special dinner that night. It was an emerald green dress with an embroidered red rose over the heart. I wonder what happened to that dress."

I took a walk down the quays under a sunless sky. It took less than thirty minutes to reach Grafton Street, but I couldn't get in the door of his shop. Through the window I saw him fitting a hat on a lady who should have known better. Darren Pringle was not as bright and handsome as his appearances on daytime TV might suggest. It was obvious he wasn't wearing his paint and powder.

His age was hard to guess because plastic surgery tends to make a man look younger. He could have been thirty, or he could have been sixty. Whatever he was, Jane was too young for him.

I sat at home that night waiting for the call. When the doorbell rang, I knew she wasn't going to call. She told me to turn off the light. Colleen Murphy, or whoever she was, was one step ahead of me all the time. She sat and refused coffee. Then I noticed she was wearing black gloves. It occurred to me that she always wore black gloves, except on two occasions.

"Tell me about Barry Allen."

"I worked for him, nothing else. Why these questions? My husband is the killer. I hired you to find proof. Do you require more money? Is that what you're after?"

"No. Let me do it my way. What about Darren Pringle?"

"He makes dresses, pretends to be something he's not. My husband was… is his lawyer. Pringle put a lot of business his way. He was often in the house."

"What about the dress?"

"What dress?"

"The dress he fitted you for. The dress he delivered to you at noon that Christmas Eve?"

She had to think, as if recalling something that had slipped her mind. It was the first time she had hesitated. It didn't matter at that time. Maybe it had slipped her mind.

"Oh, that dress. I was wearing it when he shot me."

She spent a few minutes there and asked again if I needed more money. For the second time I said no. What I really needed was to spend a year in a Buddhist monastery in Tibet to figure things out. I was beginning to believe in all sorts of things I used to dismiss out of hand, like reincarnation. Maybe the dead do come back. Dermot Brady was dismissive. I phoned him after she'd left. I told him she knew things only the victim could have known. Brady said he knew a man who could fit a concealed camera and listening equipment in my apartment.

Dusk fell on the city, and I was parked not far from Pringle's apartment on Harcourt Street. He had done well for himself, living in a penthouse apartment in that fashionable street. From a nearby hotel, I heard music and dancing. The season was in full swing, and people were out having a good time again. Meanwhile, I was waiting as usual.

He emerged from the building and strolled across the street to an underground carpark. Minutes later a bright red Alfa Romeo speeded down the street. It was one of those Italian jobs with a black soft top, unsuitable for the Irish climate. I suspected that was the reason he'd bought it, to be different. My VW followed at a discreet distance.

Pringle led me on a familiar route down the quays; I followed at a safe distance with plenty of traffic to hide behind. I had an empty feeling in the pit of my stomach. He was heading into Smithfied. I watched his brake lights turn red, and he pulled in to park. I waited until he was out of sight. He crossed the wet cobblestones and talked to the concierge. It didn't take a genius to figure out he was going up to see Amy Reddy. Her light came on in the top floor, and then the blinds closed down. The world returned to darkness.

*

I picked out a tuxedo in a shop across the road from my apartment where I bought my shirts. They knew my size. They put it in a bag, and I took a few steps to the bookie shop. Franky Mangan was there studying form. He knew better than to ask me for a tip. So we talked about other things.

"What's with the tuxedo, Jack? Slumming, are you?"

The tuxedo was wrapped and in a bag. Franky could not have seen it, but he'd spotted me coming out of the shop and figured it out. He should have been in charge of the investigation, not someone like

Kenny. Franky had something that Kenny lacked – a brain.

"A Christmas do, Franky."

"Amy Reddy? She's out of your league. She's one of them motts who love a bit of rough on the side. She's after bigger fish like Allen. Steer clear of that mott, Jack."

"I think you should mind your own fucken business, Franky."

At home I had a shower and a shave, thinking about my response to Franky. We were friends and I shouldn't have snapped at him. I made a mental note to apologise when we next met. After drying off I selected a tie and my only overcoat. From my bedroom locker I picked out the most suitable business card. A business card opens a door closed to a private detective. 'Carlton & Sons, Stockbrokers', seemed just right. Very few people questioned a business card.

Marlborough Street runs parallel to the main city thoroughfare, and is a million miles away. It's an area frequented by druggies and addicts because the methadone clinics are centred around there. Giving methadone to an addict is much the same as weaning an alcoholic off the drink with whiskey. The druggies are usually so spaced out they could qualify as extras in a sci-fi movie about zombies. I took a taxi for safety.

An eye appeared in the door of a nondescript house. The eye had a voice, and asked what I wanted. I told the eye that a friend had recommended the club, and mentioned David Lanigan. I told the eye that I too was a stockbroker and showed it the card.

The eye was very impressed when I showed it my card, and then the door opened.

Not being an expert on Chinese interior decoration, I didn't know if the décor was Ming or Ching. There were plenty of reds and yellows, and girls. The lighting was subdued, but it could not cover the naked flesh on show. There was a bar, so I had a bottle of beer. The barman didn't blink when he asked for a twenty and no change. It was going to be a long night.

A naked girl danced on the counter. Well, she was wearing a pair of frilly garters. Now and then she stopped, and only started again when a client stuck a note in the garter. She had to go to the changing room for bigger garters.

An African girl in a G-string sat at my table and asked me for a drink, and ordered champagne. I was carrying five hundred and guessed I could not afford the champagne from Romania. So I cancelled the order and bought her a beer. Another twenty. She wasn't overjoyed and explained that she was on commission. She managed to empty the beer in a second or two, and asked for another.

I didn't know how until a saw a head of froth on a nearby flower pot. I told her that the flower had had enough for the night, so she got down to business.

"Do you want a menu?"

"I have good memory. Were you here Christmas Eve last?"

"Nobody is here that long. Two hundred for an hour with me. Five hundred for an hour with me and another girl. A thousand and you get a bottle of champagne thrown in. Of course, you can claim it as a meal from your firm. We can give you a receipt for food."

"I'll think about it."

"If you're not buying, I have to go. I'm on commission."

"It's not you I'm worried about, it's that flower there. It's had enough to drink already. It's starting to topple over."

A succession of girls came and went, all offering different services. None had been there last Christmas Eve. The turnover in staff told its own story. As midnight approached, I was on my own. The word had spread that I wasn't buying.

The woman who approached my table was built like a Tiger tank. She wore a red dress slit to the thighs, but that was her only concession to womanhood. Her arms were bigger than my legs, and she was broader at the shoulders too. When she sat at my table, I could see through the make-up.

"I am Madame Wu. Does the gentleman require some special services? We are here to please. Name your vice."

For a start, she wasn't Chinese. She had a Dublin accent you could cut with a hacksaw. She was fifty at least, and she knew the ropes. She had the type of manner that required a yes rather than a no.

"Browsing."

"Time is money. No spend, no stay."

So I put ten fifties on the table, and she smiled. She moved closer, as if I was her son. Her arm linked in mine. Her perfume was not natural. It repelled rather than attracted. Or maybe good perfume smells bad on an ugly woman.

"See that old man over there with Sasha?"

I followed the line of her eyes. He was in his seventies, and Sasha was in her teens. She was high on something, she had to be. The old man had his hand up her crotch. She was smiling, but then she was paid to smile.

"Judge Cleary," Madame Wu said. "You're safe here."

When I told her the money was for information, she clammed up. Her hand made a grab for the notes, but my hand was faster. The barman saw what was going down and came at me. He was not alone. They came out of the shadows, six bouncers who didn't want to wish me safe home. I kicked over the table and a couple of chairs to make time and ran for the door. Somebody up there must have loved me that night, because people were coming in and the door was open. The night air had never tasted so good.

*

Amy Reddy looked better than a jackpot. She was dressed in a simple blue dress, with a ring of pearls on her neck. She said they were false. They looked better on her than the real thing. Genuine pearls could not have matched her flawlessness.

We took a taxi to the Gresham Hotel. The room was starting to fill up by the time we arrived. The ballroom had a bar at the top, and white-coated waiters and waitresses to ferry the drinks.

A few men were at the bar getting tanked up. We sat at a table for four, and I ordered two whiskies.

"Who's joining us, Amy?"

"Paul Murphy and Sharon Cook. And before you sulk, I did not make the arrangements. Remember, Jack, it's for charity. Forget business for one night."

I'd been warned, be on my best behaviour. Amy had one drink, but I had a couple more. A band played Smoke Gets in Your Eyes. We danced. It had been a long time since dancing with a woman I wanted to dance with. Her arms found my neck and her breasts found my chest. The song should have lasted five minutes, but it was over in seconds.

The missing couple were at the table. Murphy was drinking a brandy and Sharon champagne. She had a rock on her finger bigger than the iceberg that sank the *Titanic*. The conversation went over my head. I answered the questions in monosyllables. I didn't love Murphy and he didn't love me. He could pretend to love me, but I could not pretend to love him. Amy was pouring oil over troubled waters, keeping up the conversation. I was happy when a waiter said there was a phone call for me at the reception desk.

"Christmas Eve is the anniversary of my death, Jack. If we go out to the house, I can give you proof he killed me. I read about his engagement in the papers. He'll kill her too."

"How did you know I was here?"

"Do I need to repeat myself? The dead know everything. I did not call on your mobile phone because of your charming girlfriend. Cancel everything for that night. Let us avenge my murder by putting him where he belongs, behind bars."

I went outside for a smoke and stood on the top step. People were out on the town. They were having a good time. I was supposed to be having a good time, but I was wondering how she had known where to find me. Someone bumped into me and I turned to say sorry. It was Murphy, and he had Lanigan with him.

"Imagine, a criminal with a classy mott," Murphy said. "She must have felt sorry for the little prick."

"Couldn't have been his good looks," Lanigan said.

"Maybe she loves dogs," Murphy laughed.

Sure, I snapped. Murphy had it coming. I hit him first and he went down. Lanigan was on my back and I couldn't shake him off. Murphy was squealing like a stuck pig. Then a shower of hands tore us apart. Murphy's nose pumped blood like a Texas oil well.

My ego was not damaged this time.

"I'll sue your ass off!" Murphy screamed.

"Sue, I'm not the State. I have no money."

CHAPTER NINE

Dermot Brady had no sympathy for me. I tried to explain my side of the story but he wasn't listening. He said I should have walked away. He was right. I wasn't thinking about myself. Amy was on my mind. I'd ruined her night. I'd had to put her in a taxi and send her home alone. I felt lower than a snake's belly.

"You'll get jail this time, Jack. You have form."

"It might ease my conscience."

"He has friends in high places. You'll get six months."

"Enough with the lectures. What are you doing Christmas Eve? It's important. I need you to tail us."

"Staying home with the wife and kids."

I turned off the mobile phone. To get the incident out of my mind, I took a tram to the Internet café to do some research on the gun. Anything to keep my mind occupied. I bought a large box of chocolates for the waitress. We were on first-name terms at that stage. She found what I was searching for.

The gun on the screen was a work of art, until I reminded myself it had been designed to kill. It was the primary hand weapon of the German Army during WW2. The Mauser threw a 7.63x25mm slug, and could be adapted for use as a rifle. The Americans sent many home as war booty, but the Europeans destroyed them, apart from the ones smuggled home by returning soldiers.

It was Christmas Eve, and the whole city was going out on the town. The time had passed ten, and I was at home getting into dark pants and sweater. We accidentally bumped into each and I stopped her falling down. Her body was warm, not cold. She wore a black woollen cap and a black jumpsuit. I had my phone in my pocket and a microphone taped to my body, supplied and fitted on the previous day by a contact of Brady's. I was going out fully prepared for anything that might happen.

We took my car and I drove. I had to be careful because revellers were spilling out on the road. I estimated the journey would take an hour at least. I checked the mirror for some unknown reason.

Perhaps I'd hoped Brady was following. He was at home with his wife and kids.

"He's not out here?"

"No, he's in town with his fiancé having dinner."

"So the place is deserted? What about keys?"

"I have keys."

Killiney was lit up, and fireworks cascaded across the night sky. The sea below us reflected their lights briefly. The car moved slowly and steadily. It passed a green telephone kiosk, standing and not vandalised. They were almost extinct around the city. We approached the house and she pointed to a dark lane where I could park the car. It wasn't far from the gates, less than a hundred metres.

Before exiting, I checked the road. It was clear. She handed me the keys to the gates, saying she'd catch up later. The house was isolated, and I opened the gates, fireworks occasionally lighting the darkness.

Walking up to the house, I noticed she wasn't nearby. I called her name softly, without reply. It took some minutes to find the key to the front door. The house was in darkness. Then a beam of light stuck me harder than a bolt of lightning. My heart stopped. She was inside the house, holding a finger to her lips and a torch in her left hand. A strange sensation coursed over my body, and then ceased, followed by numbness. My body felt dead from the neck down. I followed the beam of the torch to a grandfather clock. The time was past midnight. A large spiral staircase wound its way to the next floor. She shone the beam on the marble steps, and I followed the beam.

The corridor was wide, with portraits on the wooden-panelled walls and statues on stands. She indicated that I had to steer wide of the statues. She stopped at a door, silent, gesturing me to open it and go inside. That's the last I remember about Christmas Eve. The excruciating pain in my head was followed by a sense of relief, and I fell into a dark place where there was no more pain.

I awoke in a palace of lights with a chandelier overhead and the flash of million cameras. My head had a man inside with a hammer trying to smash my brain. My breath tasted of stale whiskey. I tried to recall the last time I'd drank whiskey, but my memory wasn't working. I was aware of something in my right hand. It was a pistol.

It was the same pistol I'd seen on the Internet. Nothing was making an ounce of sense.

A lot of people were standing over me. Superintendent Kenny had a grin wider than a basking shark. Dermot Brady was concerned.

Nobody was saying anything, but I was in trouble. A cop in a white outfit removed the gun from my hand, using gloves. Two more cops lifted me to my feet. My legs were made of jelly. I was standing over a bed with red sheets. Except they weren't red. The sheets were covered in blood. It wasn't a Hollywood movie where the blood resembles tomato ketchup. Real blood can't be faked.

"How did you get in?" Kenny demanded.

"Keep your mouth shut, Jack," Brady advised.

"You keep out of this, detective," Kenny said.

"He has his rights," Brady said.

"I am ordering you!" Kenny threatened.

"You're not at home now," retorted Brady.

"What do you mean by that remark?" Kenny asked.

"We both know what I mean," Brady said.

They argued the rights and wrongs of the law. At one stage, they were head to head. Brady clearly was in the mood for a fight. They were coming to blows until a man in a white coat stood between them. My legs were shaky and it took two cops to keep me standing. I saw a body in the bed, then two. A team of forensic scientists was cordoning it off the bed in blue tape. Paul Murphy had a bullet hole in his head.

He was dead. I thought Sharon Cook was dead too because she was covered in blood. She was trembling too much to be dead. A doctor stood over her with a syringe, probably to knock her out. One person dead in the bed and another in total shock. It was Christmas Day.

The food wasn't bad for a police cell. There was turkey and sprouts, and a selection of potatoes. I could have had roast, boiled, or mashed. There was gravy too. I had no appetite, and the taste of whiskey lingered on my breath. I tried to retrace the events of the previous day, and could not recall taking a drink. A young guard came to take away the uneaten food.

"Not hungry?" she asked.

"No. Where am I?"

"Kevin Street garda station. Happy Christmas."

"What time is it?"

"Twelve-thirty."

I had no watch on my wrist and no phone in my pocket. Then I remembered the bugging device. There was a splotch of red on my chest, but no device. I tried to catch some sleep but my head ached too much. The young guard brought me a couple of aspirin and a glass of water.

"Do you have my watch or phone?"

"They weren't on you when they took you in."

"What time was that?"

"The desk sergeant logged you in at four-ten."

An hour or two later Brady appeared and came into the cell.

I was expecting a lecture but he said nothing. He asked me to tell him everything that happened. I reran the night as best I could. I told him about the taste of whiskey in my mouth, but that I hadn't been drinking.

"You don't recall blowing into the bag? There was enough alcohol in your blood to knock down an elephant."

"No, but I hadn't been drinking."

I rolled up my sweater and showed him the blotch where the bugging device had been taped. He said there was nothing on me when they put me in the cell. No watch, no phone, no bugging device. My brain refused to work.

"How is the girl, his fiancé?"

"In a complete state of shock. She remembers little of the night except the shot that woke her up. She saw a dark figure standing over her in the bed, but she couldn't give a description. Better hope this case doesn't go to court. Right now she is your worst enemy. Keep that in mind."

"Me? I didn't kill him."

"I'm talking a jury here. I'm talking a beautiful young girl like her on the stand. Think about that. Her fiancé murdered in his sleep? And she at his side? You're found drunk at the scene with the murder weapon in your hand? And you after giving him a hiding a few days before the murder in front of dozens of people who can identify you? Guilty as charged."

"Colleen Murphy murdered him."

"Colleen Murphy is dead. Did you get the fingerprints?"

"She was wearing gloves, Dermot."

"Smarter than you, obviously. Kenny is bound to be in soon. It's Christmas Day, but he'll have made sure reporters are on the scene. Tell him nothing. Keep dumb. Play it smart for once in your life. Meanwhile, I'll see if I can get you out."

The commotion outside suggested Brady had been right as usual. Superintendent Kenny was holding court on the steps of the station. A media scrum of reporters and TV crews sought his every word. Kenny was dressed in his light blue uniform. He had a pair of light brown leather gloves, and his shoes reflected the pale light.

"One question at a time, please."

"Did Russell murder him?"

"In our system of justice, every man is innocent until convicted by twelve jurors of his peers. I have left my wife and children to come down here today because it is my duty as an officer of the law. The welfare of the citizens of Dublin is my primary concern. One more question."

"Why did he do it?"

"That, madam, is a leading question."

The young garda blushed and showed him to the cell. Before he sat, he whispered in my ear: "Fucking scumbag, I'll make sure you'll never see the light of day again." Then he smiled and sat down, and asked: "Well, Mr Russell, I do hope we are treating you well. Anything I can get to make your brief stay here more comfortable?"

The young guard returned to her duties.

"Better to confess to me now, Russell. You have no defence. You attacked the unfortunate Paul Murphy before you murdered him and I can prove it. There are witnesses to the assault, and there is a witness to the murder. Well, what have you to say for yourself? You were always a violent thug."

There was a spot on the wall. I stared at the spot. I was about to ask what witness he had, until I recalled Brady's advice. I kept dumb. It was the most difficult time of my life.

"Are you associated with a criminal by the name of Francis Mangan, otherwise known as Franky? He is fifty-one years old and he has spent ten of those behind bars. He was charged with, and prosecuted for, robbery at Paul Murphy's house. I can prove he robbed the Mauser gun from the house and supplied it to you. The same weapon that you used to murder the sleeping man and traumatise his fiancé."

Sure, I wanted to scream I didn't kill them, but for once I was playing it smart. I was looking at a life sentence otherwise.

"I always knew you were a bad egg. That's why I had you thrown out of the force."

We did have history. It wasn't a good history either. He kept goading and goading. I kept staring and staring. He was getting nowhere fast and beginning to redden up. The young guard came to the cell with a telephone. She said there was a woman on the line named Amy Reddy. I told her to say I was sleeping.

I spent a few days in the cell before Brady had me released under his supervision. Maybe it was the season, or maybe he'd found a sympathetic judge.

The bail was set at ten grand. I didn't have that sort of money but Brady went guarantor. I had to surrender my passport, but I was going nowhere. Now I was working for myself.

On January tenth, in the rain, I took Jane out for a burger and chips. I had an envelope in my pocket, the balance of the money given me by the corpse. I think there was a couple of grand inside. It was meant as a redundancy payment.

"You'll need it yourself, Jack."

"No, take it. Find another job."

"Tell you what, I'll work it off. We need to go through the files. Maybe we can find who set you up, and why. Anyway, you can't live on fresh air. You have to earn money."

"Ok, I wasn't thinking straight."

"Let me do the thinking until you get your head back in order. I'll reopen the office tomorrow morning."

CHAPTER TEN

It might sound like an oxymoron, but your competitors are your friends. They're your friends because you have most things in common with them. You're in the same business, with the same problems. You can talk about things other people don't understand.

I never appreciated this concept until the phone in my pocket rang. Jane had left the burger place, and I was on the third container of coffee. Tom Dalton was a private detective who specialised in marriages. During the boom, a lot of mem and women had become rich in Dublin. Rich men and women have a habit of attracting more potential partners than poor men and women for some unknown reason. That's where Tom came in. Men hired him and women hired him to sort out the gold-diggers from the others, like wheat and chaff. Tom wasn't sexist, he treated both equally.

"Jack, I've been trying to contact you."

"The office was closed, but it'll be back in operation from tomorrow. My mobile was stolen. What can I do for you?"

"That what happened? I've been ringing it since I

heard you were arrested. No response. I rang Brady and he gave me this number. Can we meet? It's three now. How about an hour in Davy Byrne's. I'm buying."

Tom Dalton was in his late sixties but looked much younger. It probably had something to do with the fact that he didn't drink or smoke. He also went for morning runs when I was turning over for another forty winks. Tom had taken early retirement and set up a detective agency. He was the sort of man who instilled trust by his easy manner. He lived a settled life and had that aura of dependability I lacked.

We sat in the back of the pub over sandwiches. The salmon was fresh but I wasn't in the right mood. There were too many questions in my head and too few answers. Tom began the conversation.

"I owe you an apology, Jack. Don't know where to begin, really. It's never happened me before. I was taken for a sucker by the woman."

"The beginning is a good place to start."

"Some months ago, October in fact, a woman came to me. She told me she was getting married and wanted me to suss out her future husband, without his knowledge, of course. Mine is that sort of business. If a decent man discovers his future wife has been checking up on him, he'll run a mile. Same goes for a decent woman, by the way. There are lots of gold-diggers out there, you know…"

"Sure. Who was the prospective husband?"

It took him a minute to answer. "You."

The pub went quiet, or perhaps my ears didn't

work. My eyes saw people's mouths moving but they made no sound. The pub was quieter than a midnight cemetery Then slowly the sounds returned, and I heard voices again. A glass tingled as a barman filled a pint.

"Me? Tom, I've had enough surprises already."

"Hear me out. I was also surprised when she mentioned your name. I vouched for you personally, but she wanted to make certain. Well, she was paying big money, and it was quiet, and I thought, what harm?"

He opened his wallet and took out a picture of the woman. It was Colleen Murphy. She wasn't deathly in the picture, but healthy. Her complexion was rosy and bright. Her hair was styled differently, but it was the same colour. There was nothing in the picture to indicate where it had been taken, just a green background of fields.

"I'm sorry, Jack. She fooled us both. She came across as nice and genuine, but in this business you can't ever be certain of anything. I'll co-operate with the guards, of course. Anything I can do to make amends."

"Did she give a name and address?"

"Maria Norman, probably false. No address."

"Phone number?"

"She always rang me on my office line. Her number never appeared. I think she was ringing from a phone box, maybe from the General Post Office. There used to be a bank of telephones down there. Maybe they're still there."

One word kept ringing in my ears on the way

home. Why? Why had she gone to all the trouble and expense? Why had she killed Murphy? Why had she framed me? I'd never met her before she'd walked into the office. Why me? Other things were far easier to figure out. Now I knew how she had contacted me at the Gresham Hotel. Tom had been trailing me. That's how she had acquired my mobile number too. The pieces fell into place before my eyes. That's how she had managed to evade Jane at the office. Jane was a creature of habit, and went to the toilet in a pub across the street at four every day. The downstairs toilet in the building didn't work properly. It was the perfect window of opportunity to meet me without Jane meeting her.

"Did you supply keys for Murphy's house?"

"God, no, Jack. That would be breaking the law."

"Or supply her with details of the house?"

"Of course not."

Early next morning, with mists were rising over the sleeping city, I hauled myself out of bed. My head ached and my bones were sore, and I'd been suckered worse than a teenage kid with a woman of the world. I consoled myself that I wasn't alone. She'd suckered Tom Dalton too. The tea tasted worse than stagnant bog water. I spent an hour in the shower and didn't consider the price of water.

It was afternoon before I made it to the office. Jane had bought a tablet and was transferring files. The old computer was a dinosaur, and slower than an Italian football team with a goal in the bag and an hour to play. She said the tablet was ten times faster with a much better memory. I think she called it progress.

"Remember that Scally case, Jack? The husband tripped over a step and claimed he suffered from vertigo? If he went on an escalator he got dizzy and fell down? Put in a claim for fifty grand?"

"I remember. Said he got nose bleeds if he stood on a chair to change a light bulb. Why?"

"Until you snapped him at the top of a ladder painting a three-storey building. Well, didn't his wife storm in here and threaten to get you? She had a holiday planned in Thailand for the whole family with that money, which she didn't get. They had to holiday in rainy Kerry instead and listen to them terrible accents."

"They'd hardly frame me for murder over a bad holiday and Kerry accents, Jane. I'm a small-time operator. I haven't stepped on any big toes that I'm aware of. Any calls?"

"A woman named Anne Neary."

"I'll see her at ten on Friday morning."

Then I asked her to do research on make-up props for TV shows and movies. They were available online. The woman who claimed to be Colleen Murphy could have bought creams to make her resemble a dead woman. She could have bought a latex prop to resemble a bullet hole too. I asked Jane to phone any store in the city supplying these products. Maybe a shop had supplied her.

Jane found two shops in the city supplying props for the film and TV industries. I visited both. Neither had any record or recollection of the woman. The picture I passed around rang no bells. The woman might have purchased the props on the Internet, but there was no way of checking that.

David Lanigan and Philip Grogan were running scared.

There was a killer on the loose. Lanigan hired a lawyer and went to a police station. The lawyer explained that his client wished to change his statement. Mr Lanigan had been drinking a lot on the day Colleen Murphy was murdered. On sober reflection, he had left the club with his two friends at three in the afternoon. They had parted outside the club and gone their separate ways.

Philip Grogan, too, went to a police station to change his statement. He asked for police protection. Obviously he thought he might be next on the list. The threat of death had forced him to tell the truth. It must have been a unique sensation for him. So far the cops had not come up with a motive for the death of Paul Murphy. To catch the killer, they'd have to first find that motive.

Brady gave me this information as we sat on a seat beside the Royal Canal. A couple of kids nervously fed swans, watched by their parents. It wasn't all good news. I knew by Brady's manner that he had something on his mind. He wasn't a man who could conceal his feelings.

"Did you happen to notice CCTV cameras that night Murphy was killed? There were two mounted above the front gates. Another two were overlooking the front door. Well?"

"It was dark."

"You drove out there before, didn't you?"

"Sure, but I didn't notice cameras."

"Stick to insurance scams in future, if you have one."

The swans climbed up on the bank of the canal and the kids did a runner. The parents picked up the kids and left. I watched the swans return to the canal in silence. Their parents had recognised the dangers that the swans presented. I had failed to recognise the danger the women known as Colleen Murphy presented.

"Why did you lie to me, Jack?"

"I didn't lie."

He considered my answer. Time stopped.

"We viewed footage of from the cameras at the front gates. The cameras were actually working, unlike most of them you see. They picked up footage of you opening the gates. You were alone."

I had to think back, to recall the events of the I didn't want to recall. Slowly, they came back to me. I had been trying to forget that night. Now I was forced to remember. It was either that or spending the rest of my life behind bars.

"She gave me the keys and told me to open the gates. I don't know where she went. Same thing at the front door. She was inside the house when I entered. Thought I told you."

"No, if you did I'd have remembered. I have been trained to remember. That's why I'm a professional and you're a bloody amateur. That's the difference between us. What the fuck did you get yourself mixed up in?"

Sure he was mad. He had every right to be mad. More silence followed. Even the swans seemed to have stopped dead. Patches of ice lingered at the edges of the canal. I stared at them silently.

"Okay, she knew the layout of the house," he eventually said, when he'd cooled down. "She knew how to avoid the cameras. Whoever she is, or whatever her motive, she'll be tough to catch. Are you sure you haven't neglected anything else? Kenny wants to take me off this case."

"I need your help, Dermot."

"Okay, I'll fight him on this one."

I gave him the phial with the saliva and hair samples in a handkerchief. They had been taken in a pub, and I recalled that she hadn't worn gloves that night. I ran the events of that night in my head over and over again sitting on the bench. She had not worn gloves that night. Perhaps she had left a fingerprint on the phial. Maybe she wasn't infallible after all.

"Swear you weren't drinking Christmas Eve."

"Cross my heart, Dermot."

"It's possible she poured a bottle of whiskey down your throat when you were out cold. That's what you're up against. She was meticulous in her planning. Did you cross anyone big enough to have you framed?"

"Well, I interviewed Barry Allen…"

"Allen? What's he got to do with this?"

"I don't know. He had a goon beat me up."

"Allen. If it's him, you're in big trouble."

The banging on the door in the middle of the night woke me up. I'd been dreaming colourful dreams about a beautiful woman called Amy Reddy. We'd been sipping wine under a parasol down in Provence, and I was not overjoyed about the banging. Superintendent Kenny was standing outside with a couple of young guards. They seem embarrassed to be standing there, unlike Kenny who could not wipe the smile of satisfaction from his cleanly shaved features. His uniform was crisp even at that time of night.

"Sign here," he barked.

"What is it? A repossession order?"

"It's a search warrant."

"I don't have Shergar hidden here."

"Don't get smart with me, Russell. Sign."

"What are you searching for?"

"Evidence."

Since I'm generally law-abiding, apart from one conviction for violent affray, I signed the document. I stood aside and let them enter. No doubt Kenny was responsible for taking out the search warrant. He was sending a shot across my bows. He had the mind of a bureaucrat.

He threw a few questions in my direction. I played it dumb.

I just said a couple of sentences, and reminded him we lived in a democracy. It wasn't a shining light-on-the-hill democracy, but nobody could be forced into a confession. Bureaucrats hadn't managed to force people to make a confession against their will.

I think he got the message.

That little lecture didn't go down too well. He ground his teeth like a bull chewing the cud. I was not his favourite person in the world. To be brutally frank, he was not mine either.

"I'll take no lectures from an ex-con like you, Russell."

They ransacked the flat as a warning.

A couple of days later I bumped into Franky Mangan in my local bookie shop. I apologised for snapping at him and he just grinned. Our friendship was worth more than words alone. He gave me a tip for Roman Princess in the four o'clock at Fairyhouse. Then he asked me for a smoke. We went outside and lit up.

"Did you rob Paul Murphy's house?"

"Yeh. I'm a modern Robin Hood, Jack. I never rob from the poor. He was rich. I'm sorry he was killed, but not sorry for robbing him. Wealth should be shared around. Isn't that what it says in the Bible?"

"Did you see a gun in the house?"

"A gun? No, I hate guns."

Seagulls wafted on the cold wind above our heads. Across the steel-grey river, the skeletons of unfinished buildings loomed large. They were stark monuments to vanity. The vanity would return though, like a phoenix rising from the ashes.

"Barry Allen is divorced, isn't he?"

"The wife will go straight to heaven for sticking with him for twenty years, Jack. Allen is on the lookout for a woman to further his career. He's making a comeback, and he needs a bit of eye candy to win over the voters. What's up with motts, eh? A fucken bear wouldn't hug Allen, and still he can get more than his fair share of motts."

If you want to figure out any man, just examine closely what motivates him. Some men are motivated by money. Other men are motivated by love. The worst are motivated by naked power.

Barry Allen was the worst.

On Friday morning Anne Neary sat in my office. She was nervously wringing her hands. I had her figured out by now. She'd been in love with Paul Murphy. That's why she'd put on a red dress and bought me fish and chips, to convince me he hadn't murdered his wife. She still believed that. She was one of those country and western gals who stand by their man, even if that man is married to somebody else.

"I want to hire you to find his killer, Mr Russell."

"Then you don't believe I did it?"

"No, you had no motive."

I asked her to draw up a list of enemies the dead man might have had, and called Jane into the office. That would take a long time. Now she had to face reality and see Murphy in the cold light of reflection. I left both of them to work on the list.

In the afternoon I took a stroll down to Grafton Street where Darren Pringle had his shop. I wanted to ask him a lot of questions, but mainly one: why had he dated Jane? He was a celebrity and as such had a choice of models and others who wanted a share of the limelight. I reckoned he had dated Jane to pump her for information on the case.

Maybe it was a generational thing between Jane and me. She was convinced Pringle had dated her because he cared for her. She hadn't realised that social climbers cared for nobody but themselves. That's why he had dumped her, because he had sucked her dry.

He had a fashionable clothes shop where women of means shopped. There seemed to be no recession when it came to clothes. I was the only man in the shop and the looks I got from the women were not funny. A parade of young assistants informed me not too politely that I was in the wrong place. I told them it was against the law to discriminate.

Pringle didn't wish to talk to me, but I refused to leave the shop until he did. He was measuring a woman's waist and I stood at his side, talking to him in a mirror. He finally relented and invited me into a rear office.

"I'm Jane's employer," the conversation began.

"Oh, I thought you might be her father."

"It's not about her. You delivered a dress to a Mrs Colleen Murphy a year ago. Do you remember that day?"

"I have given all that information to the guards. Sorry, but you are not a guard. You are a cheap detective." He took out a mobile phone. "There is the door and you have two minutes. Well, what are you waiting for?"

"Why have you been pumping my secretary for info?"

He started the punch in numbers, and I suspected he was not calling the Salvation Army. I could not afford to have the cops on my back, so I left.

CHAPTER ELEVEN

Dermot Brady could not afford to be seen with me. I picked him up in a deserted factory site, and we headed for Carlow.

It was now late February, and nothing had broken in the case. Jane had turned up nothing either. Most of the insurance companies had dropped me, and I was taking work wherever I could find it. Tom Dalton was also helping me out, hiring me to do most of his legwork. The gold-diggers hadn't stopped hunting business, and I was kept occupied.

"Where we going, Jack?"

"Saint Mullins. Her family hailed from there."

He had something on his mind, I could tell that. He shifted in the front seat and toyed with the belt. It was too tight on his big body. I told him to adjust it and stop grunting. He was not listening.

"How long there?"

"Hour and a half. We'll have breakfast in Carlow."

My mobile phone rang, and I pulled into the side of the road. I couldn't afford to be seen driving and holding the phone at the same time. Brady was my friend, but he was also a cop. I needed to be on my best behaviour.

"Amy Reddy wants your number," Jane said.

"Tell her I'll contact her soon."

The journey south resumed under a wintery sky. The season was dragging its heels. The roadside trees showed no signs of recovery. They were still asleep, awaiting warm breezes from a new month. I mentioned the weather to Brady but he made no comment about the season.

"Think she's involved?"

"I don't know, Dermot. Why is she trying to contact me after I made a show of her at the ball?"

"It can't be love, surely. I took the liberty of checking up on her, just in case. No skeletons in the closet. She does a lot of charity work. Nothing to report really, except she has bad taste in men. Really bad taste."

"Thanks for the vote of confidence."

"Just can't figure what she sees in you."

We had breakfast in Carlow, bacon and eggs. He had something on his mind. He'd been edgy on the journey, unable to sit still. He unbuttoned his overcoat and took out two bulky large brown envelopes. I suspected they were not the results of a lottery win on my part.

"Okay, don't beat about the bush. What are they?"

"The results of the DNA tests."

"So? Don't prolong the agony."

He toyed with the bacon and eggs too before

pushing them aside. Then he got up and went to the toilet. The two bulky envelopes sat on the table. One was marked Exhibit A, and the other Exhibit B. He spent a long time in the toilet. By the time he returned, his tea was cold. He started to shoot questions at me like a suspect. Or maybe he was mad about the cold tea.

"Tell me about the night she gave you DNA samples."

"Told you already."

"Tell me again, Jack."

I related everything again about that night. I told how she had taken swabs from her mouth. I told how I had plucked hairs from her head. They had been placed in a phial, and I had put them in my pocket. I told him something else too. She hadn't worn gloves on her first meeting and she hadn't worn them that night either.

"There was no switch?"

"A switch? What the hell are you talking about?"

"She didn't switch the phial containing the DNA samples? Think hard before you answer. Take your time. Well?"

I thought hard. The events of that night were clear enough. They repeated in my mind, again and again. There had been no switch. She had swabbed her mouth and placed the swab in the phial. I had plucked a few strands of hair from her head and placed them in the phial too. There was no switch.

"No, Dermot. How could there be?"

"Exhibit A. These are the samples you gave me in

the phial. Exhibit B. These are samples we picked up at the home of the murdered woman, Mrs Colleen Murphy. We recovered hairs in her bedroom from a hairbrush. We sent them for DNA testing. We sent them, and we got them back."

He didn't finish the story. I was having to drag the story out of him like a bull from a boghole. I waited for a response. He was not forthcoming. Now I was beginning to doubt my best friend too.

"This fucken silence is killing me."

"They're the same."

"What!"

"The samples are identical. It's the same DNA. I thought it was a mix-up, or cross contamination. I phoned the lab and asked them to run the tests again. They came up with the same results.

The samples are the same."

"The corpse was… is Colleen Murphy?"

"So it would appear."

"What about fingerprints from the phial?"

"We did get fingerprints, but they were yours."

"What!"

"You heard me first time, Jack."

"Mine? I don't understand."

"You handled the phial instead of picking it up with a hankie. When we ran the prints through the computer, your name came up because you have a record. Kenny pressed charges against you for assault, if you can remember that far back. Therefore, you have a criminal record."

"What about her prints?"

"Nothing. She's a smart cookie, whoever she is."

Nothing was making sense. Identical DNA samples could mean only one thing in my mind. Colleen Murphy was not dead. And yet a coroner had pronounced her dead. She had been cremated and her ashes given to her husband in an urn. I was living in a world where nothing made sense.

"Think someone else was cremated, Dermot?"

"Why ask me? I'm in the dark too. Nobody identified her but the husband. He swore she was his wife. He had proof she was his wife. She was an only child, no parents or no siblings to say the dead woman was not his wife."

"She could have been anyone?"

"No, she was his wife."

"Stop playing games, Dermot. Did you take fingerprints?"

"Are you telling me my job? We took fingerprints and compared them with those found at her house. The prints matched up. We have no doubt that Colleen Murphy was the murdered woman. Logic plus the natural law of life and death dictates that the woman who hired you is not Colleen Murphy."

Fifty minutes later we pulled into the small village and parked on a grassy slope beside the cemetery. We found the grave near an old monastery, roofless and deserted. The gravestone was simple, marking the final resting place of Patrick and Brigid Dowling. It had been erected by their only child, Colleen. We silently stood there for a few moments and then departed.

"A grave can be excavated, Jack. A crematorium can't. Paul Murphy murdered his wife, and had her cremated to get rid of the evidence. If his wife had been buried, we could have dug her up and carried out more tests. Now all we have is a mystery and a woman who's supposed to be dead."

We didn't spend too long in the village. Within an hour we were back on the road. The mood in the car was silent, with no words passing between us. The weather hadn't changed for the better. It seemed to match my mood.

"Any news of my mobile phone, Dermot?"

"We obtained records from the phone company. There's a mast not far from the house. It picked up a signal from your phone shortly after eleven. After that, nothing. She destroyed it. That's why it didn't ping when she returned to the city, that's if she did return to the city."

"Have you tried to find her?"

"What for? She's committed no crime. We don't even know if she exists. She could be a figment of your imagination. You're not a stable man, Jack. Everyone knows that."

"Thanks for being on my side. I nearly forgot, you should pick up a cabbie called Mickey Flanagan. He works the Trinity College taxi rank. He gave Paul Murphy the alibi for the night Colleen Murphy was murdered. It's my guess the cabbie picked Murphy up when he drove her car up the Wicklow Mountains."

"We questioned him already."

"Do I have to tell you how to do your job, Dermot? People lie, and that's a fact. You're a cop and you must know people lie. Don't you know that?"

*

Jane had quickly forgotten about Darren Pringle, but I had not. I owed him another visit. I sat with her for an hour or two sifting through files. We could find no suspect who'd want to frame me for murder. Then I phoned Amy Reddy, and asked her out on a date. She said yes, and I wondered why.

The lighting was suitably low and the music subdued. We were in an Italian restaurant in Parliament Street, opposite City Hall. Amy was eating Tuscan chicken and I had a steak. She explained the recipe, saying that the chicken was seasoned with capers. I had to ask her what they were. She had a healthy tan from a week in the Algarve. She glowed positive. I didn't ask if she'd spent it alone.

"Don't you love Puccini, Jack?"

"Not since he fell and took my money with him."

The music too was subdued, easy on the ears. It blended well with the ambience. I was wearing a shirt and tie for a change. A sweater acted the part of a jacket. It was that sort of date, informally formal.

"It's an aria from Madame Butterfly. Do you like opera?"

"I don't understand opera."

"What's there to understand?"

"Take that opera, for example. A woman killed

herself because her lover married another woman? I can't imagine any woman in Dublin doing that. Here they'd kill him and cash in the insurance policy. Then they'd find a toyboy to splash it on."

"Ah, you're very cynical, Jack."

"Too highbrow for my tastes."

"And horse racing is?"

"Horse racing is real life, Amy. That's the difference."

She grinned and shook her head, and ate the Tuscan chicken.

I'm no connoisseur when it comes to wine, but I do believe that white wine is required when eating chicken. Her wine of choice was red. In the candlelight it appeared to glow between her hands like blood. The restaurant was warm and cosy, with an imitation coal fire throwing out heat. But a cold chill ran down my spine, and it wouldn't go away.

"Are you still under suspicion. Jack?"

"Numero uno suspect."

"Do you have any idea who the woman is?"

"No, do you?"

"Me? How should I know?"

She stared at me with those eyes. They were far too deep. A man might drown in them, or bask in their warm and welcoming pools. It was impossible to figure out how she was thinking. Either she was genuine, or the best actress on the planet.

"Just making conversation. Let's change the

subject. By the way, I apologise for my behaviour at the ball. I think you should be warned that I have a temper. I'd count to ten except I left school at an early age."

"Try not living up to your name," she advised.

She didn't say anything about small men and small dogs having a problem with their lack of height. According to the people in the know, that's why small men and small dogs get into so many fights. She talked about art and philosophy, and other things of the mind. Amy had a finely tuned brain, and I listened. The hours passed faster than minutes, and soon night changed into morning. We left the restaurant and went for a stroll in the city. We walked down cobbled streets beneath pillars of golden light shining from Dublin Castle. A slight drizzle had dampened the stones and they glowed in the lamplight. Her hand found mine.

We kissed under the lamps, and she offered to make coffee in her apartment. It was an offer of coffee, and afters. Her kiss had made that promise. However, I had to keep a clear head. It's hard to keep a clear head sleeping with a woman. A man tends to have other things on his mind. I remembered the kiss as I made my way home alone.

"You did what?" Jane said. "It's a bit late in the day to be playing hard to get. Have you looked in the mirror lately? It's not Brad Pitt staring back at you. It's a forty-odd year old man with a bald patch too. What are you waiting for, a movie star with a string of betting shops?"

It was a mistake to tell her about the date, a big

mistake. She didn't understand. She was young. The young are different.

"I can't get involved with a woman who might be pulling the strings. Business and pleasure are the same as oil and water. They don't mix. I can't afford to take that chance, Jane. Some time ago I tailed Pringle. He ended up in her apartment late at night."

"So what? That's his job. Men!"

*

Darren Pringle opened the door, and seeing me, tried to close it again. I'd bluffed my way past the security guard at the desk downstairs, using a fake business card. Pringle tried to shut me out but my foot prevented this happening. He pushed hard but I pushed twice as hard. It was late at night, and he was wearing a silk dressing gown. His chest was waxed and tanned, not a single hair to be seen. I think it was the latest fashion.

"This is harassment!"

In the background a young boy scrambled to put on his clothes. He was no more than fourteen years old. He was seated on a rug beside a glass-topped coffee table. There were lines of cocaine on the table, like drills of potatoes. He was stoned out of his young head. His eyes were glazed and he was unable to dress himself. I took off my coat and threw it over his shoulders.

He staggered to the bathroom, falling like a drunken reveller on St. Patrick's Day.

"This is private property, Russell."

"Lucky for you. That boy is under the legal age of consent."

"That's none of your business."

"Right, we can do this the easy way or the hard way."

"Go away or I shall call the guards!"

"Why don't you call the cops and make a complaint? I'm pretty sure if that young boy hiding in the bathroom is a minor. It's an offence to have sex with a minor, boy or girl. All you need do when the cops arrive is produce his birth cert. I presume he did bring it?"

It's amazing how fast the threat of jail can open a closed mouth.

Pringle lived well. His apartment had a high ceiling and fine furnishings. The fashion business paid well, not to mention the TV slots in the afternoons. He had a lot to lose if he went to jail.

I knocked on the bathroom door. The boy was crying. The door opened and I went inside. He was huddled up beside the bath. His body seemed out of control and he was unable to stop the trembling. He was too young for Pringle, and for his world.

"Are you okay to travel? I'm a private detective."

"Yeh." He nodded.

"I'm like a priest in a confessional. Nothing I see or hear is repeated. Okay? I suggest you get dressed and go home. I'm sure Darren will pay for the cab."

Pringle made the call and the young boy emerged from the bathroom and collected his clothes. Pringle was a predator, using his fame to attract victims. The boy was not the first to be bitten by the celebrity bug, and he wouldn't be the last. His actions were unsteady as he exited the apartment.

Pringle used his celebrity as a Hollywood casting couch. His face was an irresistible magnet for my closed fist. So I socked him one on the kisser for the young boy. Also as a warning of things to come if he didn't tell me the truth. He collapsed like a sack of beans, holding his jaw. Liberals say that violence achieves nothing. I bet they can't name a single country that achieved its independence by peaceful means, not one. I used violence to get at the truth. There is no more worthy cause.

"What's your relationship with Amy Reddy?"

"She's a customer, nothing else."

"Why did you date Jane?"

"To find out what you knew. Paul Murphy was my friend. I was trying to help him. That's what friends are for. Do you have any friends, Russell? I bet you have none."

"I'm asking the questions. You knew he killed his wife, didn't you?"

His refusal to answer told me what I needed to know. Paul Murphy had murdered his wife. Not that it made any difference to Pringle. He didn't know the difference between right and wrong, and didn't give a damn. As long as it didn't interfere with his cosy life, it was business as usual.

"Okay, let's talk about the day he murdered his wife. Tell me what you saw at the house that day. Did you see anyone out there apart from the victim? Any cars? If you lie, I'll beat the shit out of you and report you for child-molesting."

The threat worked. Obviously Pringle cared a lot about his plastic surgery. He didn't want it disturbed by my fists.

"She had ordered a dress from me a couple of months before. I delivered it around noon. She was alone in the house. Her car was parked outside, a white Ford I think. I wanted to fit the dress, just in case it needed any adjustments. She said she had to take a shower first. I put the dress on the kitchen table, and left."

"What time was that?"

"Somewhere between twelve and one."

"You were working that day?"

"Yes, it's one of our busiest days."

He was telling the truth, or what passed for the truth in his mind. I left him there in his plush apartment. He wouldn't report the assault to the cops. He had too much to lose.

I'd been tailing Allen for a week, losing sleep at night. It was routine stuff. Sometimes at night his chauffeur picked him up. The chauffeur wore a uniform and a peaked cap. Very few taxpayers were chauffeured around in a limousine. On Friday night he headed out of the city, driving south on the motorway. About ten miles out he wheeled left onto a narrow road. He was heading up the Wicklow Mountains.

The mountain road had no traffic and I followed at a safe distance. The Mercedes climbed in the night, its signal taillights vanishing as it rounded twisting bends. The car had two persons on board, the chauffeur and Barry Allen. I had to be careful they didn't see me and drove on the dims. The moon was out which made driving a little easier, and I kept a safe distance. I pulled in to let a delivery van pass. There was a restaurant about a mile ahead, but it wasn't frequented by many people because of the recession. It was also out of the way.

In the distance, like a beacon to ships at sea, lights turned night into day. The Mercedes swung into a gravel carpark and the taillights turned off. My VW came to a halt, and rested out of sight behind a wall. On silent feet I made my way to the carpark. In the moonlight I saw two cars parked out front. One was the Mercedes with his chauffeur asleep at the wheel. The second was a BMW. The car was blue and it had plates I recognised.

Amy Reddy was seated opposite Barry Allen and they were holding hands across a dinner table. I could see them through a window. There was a candle on the table and a bottle of red wine. A joke was shared and they both laughed. I was beginning to think that the joke was on me.

CHAPTER TWELVE

Mary Casey was picking up the broken pieces of her broken life, and getting on with her life. She was in the same boat as all the other victims of the Celtic Tiger. Sure, she had been hit harder than most, but that's life. She was young, and she had a long life ahead of her. The young are more resilient than the old. They can take the knocks that life hands out and start all over again. They have the time to start all over again.

She had a job in a newsagent's down on the quays. I went down to have a chat with her, that's if she'd chat to me. She wore a white shopcoat and her hair tied up in a bun. It was nearing lunchtime and I offered to buy her a sandwich, adding that it would be the last time she'd see me asking questions. She agreed on that condition.

We had tea and cheese sandwiches in a nearby café. Mary did not trust me, but then she was in the majority. I informed her that I was the number one suspect in the murder of Paul Murphy. I was appealing to her femininity and compassion. I think she softened up a little after that. It takes a victim to recognise someone in the same predicament.

"Did you still have locks and chains on your door?"

"Not now, no."

"You were afraid of Paul Murphy?"

"Yes. I thought..."

"His brother James was killed in a car crash. Maybe it was an accident, or maybe somebody had arranged the accident. It's happened before. So you were playing it safe with all those locks. Now you can sleep without locks."

"Something like that, yes."

"Do you think Paul Murphy killed his own brother? Was that thought at the back of your mind? Their parents are rich barristers, after all. One hundred percent of a big inheritance is better than fifty percent any day. Brothers have been killed for a lot less."

"I don't know what to think anymore."

We had no more than an hour, so I filled her in. The corpse and Colleen Murphy had the same DNA. Therefore, they were one and the same. Yet that was impossible. I asked if she had any ideas. I needed help badly.

"I met her once. James took me out to the house. She accepted me, didn't look down her nose at me. She knew I loved James. A woman knows these things. It was her husband. He wanted James to do better. He knew nothing about love."

"Did you ever see a gun out there?"

Her head nodded. "James showed it to me that day. I think he was showing off. He could be like that sometimes. It was kept in a mahogany case in the kitchen, on a high shelf near the cooker. I recoiled at the sight of that gun. He didn't mention it after that."

I showed her the picture of the corpse on the mobile phone.

She studied it for a long time before making a commitment. Then her head nodded again. There was no doubt in her mind.

"Yes, that's her, that's Colleen Murphy."

"She's supposed to be dead."

"I can't explain that."

"Did you attend the cremation?"

"No, because I wasn't wanted."

"Was James Murphy cremated?"

"He was buried in Glasnevin Cemetery."

That figured. Cremation wasn't part of the family culture. Colleen Murphy had been cremated to destroy any potential evidence. Fire has a way of doing just that. Ashes can't be forensically examined for clues.

The phone rang and Charlie Bastable asked me out for a liquid sandwich. He was in a pub around the corner. I could not refuse because he was in my corner, and I needed all the help I could get. We spoke off the record, and I replied that I was in serious trouble.

"Somebody big is out to get you, Jack."

"I can't figure out why."

"If you want my opinion, Allen is at the bottom of this. He has a minder who eats crack cocaine for breakfast the same way normal people eat porridge. He should be in jail, but Allen has a way of pulling strings. Crack cocaine has no conscience."

"What's his motive, Charlie?"

"The thug? He's a fucken sadist."

"No, Allen."

"Not good, whatever it is. Did you know he has a political dictionary? Keeps it at his bedside for handy reference. He reads it every night before nodding off. Some people prefer to read a good thriller. It's a masterpiece."

"What's a political dictionary?"

"Same as the Oxford one, except it's missing a lot of words. For example, you won't find the word 'honesty' in it, or the word 'duty'. Other words are missing too, such as 'probity' and 'integrity'. Let me see, 'loyalty' is also not in there, and 'friendship'. As a matter of fact, Jack, any word that can be vaguely connected with humanity or goodness is missing."

"I'd appreciate any help, Charlie."

Next day *The Tribune* ran a hard-hitting article stating that the murders of Paul Murphy and his wife were connected. It alleged that a very prominent politician was involved, without naming Allen. The paper was skirting around the draconian libel laws. It also alleged that the cops were trying to frame an innocent member of the public for the murders. By publishing allegations without naming names, the newspaper avoided the legal vultures working for Allen.

Early on the following morning, Jane received a call from Allen's acolyte, who asked to speak with me.

She checked if I was available, and my head shook. He'd have to wait, just as I'd had to wait in his office. Two could play at his game.

"He's not here," Jane said.

"When do you expect him back?"

"No idea, really."

"Ask him to ring Mr Allen. It's urgent."

Now the shoe was on the other foot. His secretary rang twenty times an hour. Jane promised to return her calls, and didn't. I was applying psychological pressure on the politician hoping he'd break. It was a long shot, but sometimes the outsider pays off.

I finally gave the okay to Jane to make an appointment with the politician. I was standing beside her when the phone rang again. This time his daughter was on the line. Jane informed her not too politely that Mr Russell would not attend the constituency office.

"Mr Russell insists on a meeting in this office."

"What time? Not daylight hours."

"Why not?"

"Constituency work."

"Ten tomorrow night. Tell him to be on time."

Jane smiled at her good day's work. She liked nothing better than putting another woman down. The politician had more faces than a stage actor and he was wearing one of them seated across the desk in my office. It was night and the blinds were drawn down. Jane had left a few hours previously, and we were alone. He wore a smile but it was a mask.

He had one for all occasions. The best actors have. I reckoned that's why his wife had left him. She'd married one man and ended up living with hundreds.

"What did you want to see me about, Jack?"

"I thought your daughter made the appointment."

"Some sort of mix-up. Anyway, I'm here now."

"Why are you trying to frame me?"

"Me? I hardly know you."

"Yet you had your goon beat me up. Why?"

"I had no hand, act, or part in that, Jack."

"What's your connection with Amy Reddy?"

"Passing, that's all. We meet at charity functions."

"When was the last time you met her?"

"Before last Christmas, at a charity collection."

It was a waste of time, but I had to throw a scare into him. So I told him I knew who'd killed Paul Murphy. All I needed was proof, the sort of proof that would put a crooked politician in jail for a long time, even in a country that didn't believe in jailing crooked politicians. I needed cast-iron proof that no court could dismiss. I was expecting an insider to call me with the details soon.

"I had no hand, act, or part in that murder."

"What about your goon?"

"I have no idea who you are referring to."

"By the way, every piece of evidence I have is with a friend, just in case I'm accidentally knocked down crossing the road by a steamroller. He'll ensure it gets into all the newspapers and on the TV channels. This is still a Western democracy, even if it doesn't act like one often enough."

*

At the weekend I met Brady in the Phoenix Park, grey mists swirling about our feet. He assured me that I was still at the top of the suspect parade. Kenny wasn't looking anywhere else. His reputation and future rested on my shoulders, not to mention an increase in pay and a pension to beat the band.

"Ballistics confirmed that the same gun killed both Paul Murphy and his wife. The WW2 Mauser. Old but it hadn't lost its ability to kill. We had no record of that gun. It was not used in any crime before the killing."

He was telling me something I already knew.

"I talked to Franky Mangan. He robbed that house a few times, but didn't see a gun."

"Mangan is an ordinary decent criminal. He robs and he sells the stolen loot to fences. We come down on the likes of him but not on the fences, but I don't make the rules. His sort have nothing to do with guns, unlike the present generation of mindless young thugs. There was a time when a row in a pub was sorted with fists. These days a row is sorted with guns."

"Any change in the DNA results, Dermot?"

"No, but there must be a rational explanation."

"Reincarnation?"

"I'm a cop, not a priest."

It was back to the footslog. Meanwhile, I had to earn a living to eat. Jane needed to be paid, and the horses weren't jumping any higher. So I combined working for myself with working for Tom Dalton. That arrangement suited us both. I could choose the cases, and Tom's conscience could feel a little better.

The hotel in Gardiner Street had one purpose in life: to serve its customers. Okay, it served an occasional meal and drink, but they were incidental to its main function, which was renting rooms by the hour. It didn't ask any questions, and it didn't discriminate. Couples were welcome, including men and women. It didn't discriminate on the colour of skin either, not that the law permitted that sort of thing. It was the sort of place that practised discretion, even if it couldn't spell the word.

The man behind the desk in the foyer had the build of a Sumo wrestler and the face of a pug. There was a cigarette hanging on his lip, and his shirt needed ironing. The carpet needed hoovering too, but he was reading a newspaper. That carpet would have to wait. His all-knowing glance said the words without a sound. I wasn't welcome. I was alone, and he booked rooms to couples and larger groups.

I'd trailed a couple to the hotel, a man and a woman. The law didn't interfere with consulting adults having sex, so long as both had birth certificates to prove they were adults. Except the man was married, and the woman wasn't his wife. Both, however, were of legal age and knew what they were doing. The man's wife had hired Tom Dalton to check up on her husband, and he had hired me.

His wife had taken her marriage vows literally for

reasons known only to her, and had expected her husband to do the same. He hadn't, but he'd gotten careless. He'd shower and perfume on Friday nights, telling his wife he was going out with the lads, a dead giveaway. She'd put two and two together, and hadn't come up with the wrong number. So she'd hired a private detective to find out if the lads were women.

Luckily for the wife, the Sumo wrestler was motivated by money. He would have sold his mother into white slavery for the right price. I got the proof I needed, for a price. But I did not feel good leaving the hotel. Insurance scams were one thing, but interfering with consenting adults, something else. However, I was in worse trouble than the husband. I did what I had to do, otherwise I had no future.

*

Professor Alan Jones was out for his daily constitutional, walking up Kildare Street. I was on the other side, and he waved a walking stick. I dodged the traffic and joined him.

He was on his way to the Dail to hand in a petition on behalf of people living in expensive dogboxes. People had paid a fortune for them during the boom, and now they were a fire hazard, and crumbling to bits. As usual, the taxpayer would be picking up the bill for the repairs.

"Walk with me, Jack."

We walked and we talked. He had heard about my trouble, and offered assistance. A north wind blew down the street and he held onto his hat. He was about seventy, but lively on his feet. He tugged at my arm and we halted outside the Dail.

"Were you taught about the Irish Famine at school?"

The professor seldom came directly to the point. He had to build up a case first. He liked to draw comparisons from history. I suspected that's what he was doing. He believed history was not about the past, but about the present.

"Yes. Why?"

"It was all propaganda, Jack. We were indoctrinated to believe that absentee landlords were the culprits for throwing tenants out on the road because they couldn't pay their rents. Rubbish! It was our own landlords. We are a greedy nation. Do you know why? Because greed produces wealth, and money is our god. We have no god but Mammon and the euro is his prophet."

It was pointless arguing that every society had its faults. The usual suspects had been responsible for the Celtic Tiger, not the people. The government had shared a bed with speculators, and the people, as usual, had to pay the price.

"Just look at these," he said, showing me some pictures of collapsing apartments. "No regulations during the Celtic Tiger years. It was the Wild West. Speculators got rich, builders got rich, and politicians got rich. Now the banks have gone bust, and the speculators are pleading bankruptcy."

"So is the country, Professor."

"But they're not bankrupt, Jack. They signed over their assets to their wives. They signed over their assets to their children. When all this blows over, they'll emerge and do the same again. Just mark my words. We're a nation with no memory of the past and destined to repeat our mistakes."

"Keep fighting against the dying of the light, Professor."

"Right. Just look at that shoddy workmanship. Had they no pride? I suppose the human race should be grateful they did not build the Parthenon in Athens. That has stood for two and a half thousand years. Look at the legacy these greedy builders and speculators left the country. My God, have they no ambition but to get rich quickly?"

We stood in the wind outside the Dail, and he handed the petition to a guard on duty, who promised to deliver it. He said he took a whiskey a day, and asked me to join him. I did join him, but had a coffee instead. He was one of those rare men who wanted the country to be a shining city on the hill. He seemed to forget that it was populated by human beings.

"What's this trouble you're in?"

So I explained everything I could, and he listened. He was not the sort of man who pretended to listen. He knew I was small-time, and the sort of work I did. That didn't matter to him. So I told him. He asked for more information, and he was informed that I was being framed for murder.

"Same DNA, you say?"

"Yes. Tell me the dead don't walk."

"Lazarus walked."

"This is Dublin. He couldn't walk here."

"Why not, Jack?"

"Bare feet. Too many syringes lying around."

"No, miracles don't happen here. It can be explained though, I mean the DNA. I did a bit of work in that field before I took up retirement. Have you heard of monozygotic twins?"

"Not lately."

"There are two types of twins. One type is called dizygotic. They are created when two eggs are fertilised. They are similar, but not identical. Monozygotic twins develop from one single fertilised egg. They are identical in every way, except one."

"Two individuals with the same DNA, Professor?"

"Identical DNA. Not only that, twins have long fascinated scientists. They tend to choose the same clothes. In school tests, the majority of twins score the same marks. There have even been claims that some are telepathic. One twin seems to know what the other is thinking."

"I thought no two people in the world were the same?"

"Monozygotic twins have identical DNA, but they can, however, be separated by fingerprints. No two persons in the world have the same fingerprints, not even identical twins. I hope that information is of some help."

The day got brighter and a shaft of sunlight illuminated the pub. The temperature went up a hundred degrees. I felt a heavy burden lift from my fallen shoulders. The shaft of sunlight turned the room into an illustrated medieval manuscript as it filtered through the stained-glass window. Vibrant colours of reds and greens and blues painted the stools and tables in patterns Van Gogh could not have dreamed up.

My future did not include the four walls of a lonely prison cell. Then I remembered that Colleen Murphy had been an only child. She had no sister.

"Colleen Murphy was an only child, Professor."

"An only child? Oh, I see. I can be of no use then."

"No other explanation, Professor?"

"Afraid not. Sorry."

*

Patrick Callaghan had worked in the Murphy house before the death of Colleen. After that, he'd been made redundant. I tracked him down to a large Georgian house in Merrion Square. The Celtic Tiger hadn't destroyed that part of the city. He was willing to talk, but not in the house. We met later that night in a shopping centre.

"Did they have any enemies that you can name?"

"She didn't, but he did. A man doesn't get that rich without making enemies. Having said that, he played his cards close to his chest. He made me redundant after she was killed. He hadn't paid me before he too was killed."

"Where'd you spend that Christmas?"

"In Spain on holidays. The guards checked and I showed them my passport. It came as a great shock when I heard about the murder. Exactly a year to the day after the death of his wife. Do you think it was a coincidence?"

"Any idea who might have killed him?"

"None. He did have a girlfriend, but naturally she didn't come to the house. I picked up the phone once and she was on the other end. He chewed me off for that. It happened on a weekend his wife wasn't at home."

"Anything you can give me on her?"

"Nothing, except a tinny voice. Someone young."

"It was Colleen Murphy who gave you Christmas off?"

"He was a skinflint, the rich usually are. She gave Maria and me time off to spend with our families. Apart from that, they were going through a difficult time. I think she wanted to be alone in the house with him to sort things out. The marriage was heading for the rocks, that much was obvious."

"Did you pick up any other vibes?"

"She was going to divorce him that night."

I showed him the picture on the mobile phone. He confirmed she was Colleen Murphy. There could be no mistake. He'd known her for five years. I asked about her special friends. She had none that he knew about, none that she socialised with. Generally she'd confined herself to the house.

I lit up outside the shopping centre. A passer-by said smokers caused global warming. The weather was freezing and steam came out of my nostrils like an old locomotive. I was shivering with the cold and stamping my feet to keep warm. A bookie shop across the street was open late. My luck had to change soon.

The phone call arrived that night, and I took it with mixed emotions. Amy Reddy was taking a picnic at the weekend and invited me along. Spring is not the picnicking season in Ireland. The weather is too unpredictable. Summer is much the same. This wasn't about dining out under the rainy sky. It was about something else.

"Okay. When?"

"Sunday morning. Pick you up at nine."

The office was getting a spring clean from Jane. No matter where I sat I was in the way. Spring affects lot of women. They feel the urge to clean maniacally. It doesn't affect men the same way. I informed her about the Sunday picnic, and she reminded me to remember the three golden rules. I asked her to remind me again because of my bad memory.

"Number one, never fall for a pretty kisser."

"Right. What's number two?"

"Never get involved with a client."

"What's the third, Jane?"

"Always get paid. Sorry, that should be first."

Sunday was miserable, with squalls of rain alternating with bands of sleet. She was on time and picked me up at nine. She wore a sheepskin coat and corduroy pants. Her car had spare blankets and a picnic wicker basket in the boot. She smelled of cinnamon and nutmeg, and other exotic spices from distant lands with cloudless blue skies and balmy beaches. My watch said it was a few minutes past ten when we wheeled off the motorway.

"You're very quiet, Jack."

"Admiring the scenery."

"What scenery? Nothing is visible with the sleet."

She drove along a winding road over the rising mountains. Her driving was good, slowing down where pools of ice lay in the shadows. She said we were going to her favourite place. That place was Glendalough, an old monastic settlement set in the Wicklow Mountains. She went there to relax, or so she said. Her business carried a mountain of stress.

"At least you don't get beaten up," I said.

"Mental stress is worse."

"I'll remember that next time I wake up in hospital."

She did a lot of small talk about the weather. Otherwise she was cheerful and in good spirits. The wipers worked hard to keep the windscreen clear. It was no day for a picnic. It was no day to be outdoors, especially on a lonely mountain road.

"If only we had better conditions in this country, Jack."

"Other countries get climate, we get weather."

"Very apt. I haven't heard that before."

The speedo didn't go above fifty kilometres. The road was narrow, cutting across deep valleys. Shades of clouds drifted on the hills, passing like shadows. A signpost appeared, and faded from the rear-view mirror. She was past it before I could read what it indicated.

"Talk to me about her, Jack."

"Who?"

"The woman you're carrying a torch for."

"Who says I'm carrying a torch?"

"I can read body language."

The mountain road was deserted, with nothing to disturb our progress except the occasional sheep huddling for cover at the roadside. We passed under a forest of fir trees, some felled and lying on the ground. The trees were green, I recall, in contrast to the bleak landscape.

"Trout for lunch. Hope you like fish."

"Suits me fine."

"She hurt you?"

"Skip the subject, Amy."

"I'm not the hurting kind. Remember that."

The gears changed and she swung the car into a sharp bend. It slowed to negotiate a turn into the carpark. A few cars were parked there, less than half a dozen. She stopped the engine and I exited to stretch my legs before lifting the basket from the boot. She unfurled an umbrella and cleaned water from a bench near an old church. She laid out the table with cutlery under the umbrella.

"Have you located the mystery woman yet?"

"Still working at it."

"What is she after?"

"Beats the hell out of me."

A couple of tourists strolled by and exchange pleasantries, cameras dangling from their necks. They strolled to the round tower to take pictures. They were American tourists judging by their accents. One woman confirmed their origins, saying she was from Arizona. She loved the weather. The sun in Arizona was too hot to bear. I suggested a swop, her climate for our weather.

Amy unpacked the basket. Two bottles of wine, one of each, were placed on the blanket. Amy didn't use paper plates but good china. I thought of all the washing up she'd have to do. She prepared the meal. The trout looked delicious and pink, steaming in the cold air. She had potatoes in their jackets, and vegetables wrapped in silver foil. She had gone to a lot of effort preparing the picnic.

"What's your connection with Barry Allen?"

"I beg your pardon? Where did that come from?"

"Well?"

"That is none of your damn business, Jack."

"I'm accused of murder and it's not my business?"

"Have you been following me?"

"I've been following Allen."

"Jumping to the wrong conclusions too, I see."

"What way am I supposed to jump?"

"What did you see?"

"Allen and you playing handsies."

"Now you've become a Peeping Tom?"

"I'm trying to stay out of prison, Amy."

"Am I a suspect? Forget it."

"Whose side are you on anyway?"

"Fuck you, Jack."

She said it like she meant it to sound. The whole world understands that word. The journey home was spent in silence. It lasted twice as long as the journey out.

CHAPTER THIRTEEN

There is a golden rule that applies to the streets of Dublin: if you see a row going down, walk on by. It could be a row between a husband and wife. In that case, both are likely to turn on you. It could be a row between druggies. In that case, you could be stabbed by a needle.

There was a row going down in a laneway opposite the Abbey Theatre. It's a place where bins of waste are left out for collection. There are pubs and restaurants in the area. I was walking on by until I heard a voice in pain. I recognised the voice. That's the only reason I ventured into the lane.

A big man was beating up on a small man. I recognised both of them. One was Franky Mangan, and the other was Allen's goon. Franky was a gambler, not a fighter. He believed in talking his way out of trouble whenever possible. But he wasn't talking himself out of this trouble. He was taking a hell of a beating.

A metal bin was convenient to my hands. I hit the goon over the head with the bin. It dented the bin but not his thick head. A second blow knocked him over. I felt good after that. It made up for the beating.

Franky seized his opportunity and took to his heels.

I knew where he'd be, in the nearest pub. A cold pint was the panacea for all his troubles. He had a big swig first before tidying himself up, glancing in a mirror behind the bar. Then he cleaned himself up in the toilet, cleaning the blood from his face. It didn't take too long. Franky wasn't a male model. He was not too interested in his looks.

"Lucky you came along, Jack. I'd have killed that fucken baboon if you hadn't come along. I'd have beaten seven sorts of shit out of him. He's a lucky fucker."

"I saw that."

"I'd be up for murder only for you."

"True. What was it about?"

"A private detective who happens to be my friend."

"Me? What are you saying?"

"He wanted to find out what you were up to, why were you hanging around with Amy Reddy. I told him to go fuck himself. He took offence at that answer. I must have insulted his manhood."

He soon forgot the beating and asked for a tip. I could not pick a winner myself, we both knew that. But backing horses is not a logical pursuit. There is a chance that even the most persistent loser can get lucky one day. It's called gambling, and every gambler knows the rules.

"Flat season starting soon," he observed.

"The sooner the better. Coolmore has a good string this year according to the papers. I've picked out a certainty for the Derby. I can't wait for the new season. This jumping favours the bookies."

"Never believe what you read in the papers, Jack."

Meanwhile, Brady was putting his job on the line by helping me. I was the prime suspect. He picked me up and we drove out to the scene of the crime. He told me that he was bringing out the killer to the scene of the crime, and had a chuckle. I didn't think it funny.

"I can cover myself if Kenny objects," he explained. "You know, confronting the criminal with the scene of the crime. Hoping his conscience will get the better of him, that's if he has one. Is your conscience bothering you?"

He opened the locked gates and pointed out the CCTV cameras I'd missed. The house was about five hundred metres distant, with turrets and overlooking the sea. Suddenly, I was colder than usual. I had to shut out the memories of Christmas Eve, although the nightmares hadn't gone away.

A couple of cops were posted at the house. Brady stopped and had a chat with one, gesturing in my direction. Again, he pointed out CCTV cameras I'd missed. He was telling me, not too subtlety, that I was an amateur to this game. I should have stuck to insurance scams.

The house looked much different in daylight. I followed him to the kitchen, tiled in light blue. It had windows with a view of the sea, and every conceivable gadget. He opened the drawers one by one, and the cupboard, although I suspected he'd been through them a dozen times before. That was his way, methodical to the point of boredom.

Following in his footsteps up the stairs, the events of that night came flooding back, as if released from a cage. I recalled the way the corpse had walked, like a cat. She'd been light on her feet, wearing sneakers. Her movements had been slinky, as if she'd been an athlete in her young age.

"Coming back?" Brady said.

"Some events, sure."

"Trauma has that effect, Jack. The brain is a mysterious organ. It shuts down sometimes, blocks memories. I guess it's a way of dealing with the trauma. I suppose we couldn't go on otherwise."

My mind returned to the night of the killing. Perhaps I'd forgotten something, however insignificant. I recalled her inviting me to the bedroom door. I couldn't recall the couple in the bed. She'd zapped me before that. She must have hit me with the butt of the gun, or something harder.

"Did you recover the bullet, Dermot?"

"It was lodged in his brain. We also found traces of linen in the wound. We suspect the killer wound it around the muzzle to deaden the sound. There were fireworks going off that night, so the killer was extra careful. This murder was planned down to the last detail, including the fall guy."

"The bullet came from the Mauser?"

"Where else? We checked up on the grandfather. He was in the British Army during the war. That's where the gun came from. Most of that stuff wasn't declared. It was put away and forgotten about. Except in this case, of course."

The bed was there where Paul Murphy had been killed. It was bare now, with no mattress or bed linen. A spray of blood painted the wall in confetti. I recalled his lifeless body, and his fiancé beside him terrified with fear. Brady went about searching the room again. There were two large wardrobes in the bedroom, his and hers. He went though both of them, searching the pockets of jackets, examining the shoes. He picked up a paper bag with an embossed name: Darren Pringle Creations. He opened it up and removed a green dress, wrapped in a pink ribbon.

"Has that dress a heart sewn on it?"

"It has. Why, what's the significance?"

"She said was wearing it when her husband shot her."

"Obviously not if it's here."

"What was she wearing?"

"A white wedding dress. What are you getting at?"

"I'll let you know when I find out."

*

A man gets to know who his friends really are when he's in trouble. It's an old cliché, but a true one. Charlie was in the office when I returned. Jane and he were having a laugh over something. It had to be a dirty joke the way they laughed.

"I dug up something that might interest you."

They were pictures of a funeral. He said they were taken at the cremation of Colleen Murphy at Glasnevin Cemetery. The mourners were dressed mostly in black. I recognised her husband and a few others. Charlie kept the last picture in his hand. When I'd gone through the rest, he turned it over. It was a blow-up of one of the mourners. She had lifted the veil to dry her eyes and that's when the shot was taken. Her features were clearly visible.

"Recognise her, Jack?"

"Colleen Murphy!"

"Attending her own funeral. There's a precedent."

"What the hell is going down here?"

"Beats me too. Look at it this way, if she was alive at the funeral, who did they burn that day?"

"Can I hang onto these?"

"If they'll help. Some more here might be of interest."

CHAPTER FOURTEEN

Sharon Cook took the killing of her fiancé very badly indeed. She dressed in sackcloth and ashes. She cried her eyes out. She sold her sob story to the redtops here and across the Irish Sea. She had the grace to charge them the going rate for celebrities, and now she was one. How a cruel and callous murderer had robbed her of the chance of happiness with the only man she'd ever loved! After two days of mourning, Sharon got back to doing what she did best: having a great time. The black dress was dumped in favour of yellows and ochres, and bright polka dots. The killing of her fiancé had done wonders for her career. The top fashion designers beat a path to her door. Sharon had a good figure and was prepared to show it, for the right price.

I tailed her from nightclub to nightclub, with a succession of young men drawn to her flame. She favoured men who wore their shirts open to the waist, with waxed chests and sleek hair. She liked young men in black leather pants. She drank vodka cocktails and danced to rap music. She never went to bed before three a.m. and never got out of bed before noon. She seldom left her apartment with the same man on her arm.

The cops had ruled Sharon out of their enquiries. She had not been married to Paul Murphy, she'd been engaged to him. If she'd been married to him, she'd have been entitled to all his possessions on his death. That's what they call motive. As his fiancée, she was not entitled to anything after his death. That is called lack of motive. The cops concluded therefore that she was not implicated in the death of her fiancé.

Anyway, she could remember little about the killing. They had gone to bed early for her, around eleven. A noise had woken her up. She recalled something running down her face. It was blood but she hadn't known it then because the room was dark and she couldn't see. A torch had blinded her too. She had been aware of one figure in the room, but could not recall whether that figure was male or female. She told the same story over and over again, so it had to be true.

Straws are not the best things to clutch at but that's what I was doing. Kenny called me in a couple of times to answer a few questions, saying it was routine. He wanted me to confess to a murder someone else had committed. He wasn't interested in the mystery woman, believing I was throwing him a red herring.

The dead don't come back, he told me. If the case went to court, I was in deep trouble. I knew that Kenny was building up a case. Circumstantial evidence might be good enough to send me down. So I asked Jane to book a B&B in the village where Colleen Murphy was born, Saint Mullins. Maybe I could find some answers there. An hour later she came into the office.

"I booked two rooms, Jack. I've been working like a dog and I need a break. Anyway, I need to talk about my new boyfriend."

I think she needed to talk because I'd been right about Pringle. That gave me no pleasure. Jane was young and had been easily taken in by his celebrity. So I didn't object too much when she booked that second room.

We set out on Saturday morning. The car was running okay now, starting on the key. She told me about her new boyfriend. He was a year older, which was good. He wanted to shack up with her, which was bad. She needed to get to know him better. She was hearing in the passenger seat, but I can't say if she was listening.

Over a coffee, we studied the pictures Charlie had given me of both funerals – Colleen Murphy and her husband Paul. She had been cremated, but he'd been buried. She pointed out Amy Reddy at the latter's funeral, dressed in black. Allen was there too, at her side, an arm conspicuously around her shoulders where the cameras could pick it out. In the background I saw a woman standing alone. She looked like the woman who claimed to be Colleen Murphy. I pointed out the figure to Jane.

"Have a peek at these two pictures. Is that the same woman in both of them? I think they're the same."

"Seems to be. Is that the corpse?"

"She wore that black outfit the first time I saw her."

"What's she after?"

161

The question hung in the air like a bird of prey. I didn't know the hell what she was after. I didn't know why I'd been set up. She had planned the murder with meticulous care. Why? I wasn't an important person.

In every small community in every small town and village in the world, there is folk memory. It's not the sort of news that merits a column in a newspaper, or an item on TV or the radio.

It's the sort of stuff that gets handed down from generation to generation. Its basic principle is the belief at happenings in a local community, however small, is much more important than global events of greater magnitude. For example, the death of a local person is more significant than the deaths of thousands of unknowns in distant lands. That's what I was after in the small village – local knowledge.

We cleaned up and had dinner, sharing a bottle of red wine. She had something on her mind. It would come out soon enough. Meanwhile, I enjoyed the food and the wine. We had lamb chops topped with sprigs of parsley, and colcannon.

"Amy Reddy rang."

"Looking for me?"

"No, to talk with me, Jack. She wanted to know why you have a chip on your shoulder over women."

"Didn't know I had. What did you tell her?"

"I told her you're a sucker for a pretty kisser, but you've been kicked so often in the teeth that you're thinking of turning gay and buying a handbag. Well, a man of forty-plus who isn't married? People do tend to talk."

"Thanks for the vote of confidence."

"Charlie Bastable told me anyway, so there's no need to act the strong, silent type. He told me about Patricia, how you were in love and planned to live happily ever after. You were in the cops at the time with a steady job. Except Patricia was after a man with ambition, and you had none. So she hitched her wagon to a cop with ambition, whose name was Kenny. He's a superintendent now, and you're scraping a living."

"Charlie should mind his own fucken business."

"Patricia was a fool, Jack."

The owner came to the table to clear up and I ordered a second bottle of wine. I asked about Colleen Murphy, née Dowling. She remembered the family. They were all dead now – mother, father, and daughter. Colleen had been murdered in Dublin, and they hadn't found the killer.

"I think her husband did it," she said. "What goes around, comes around. Not that I'd wish that on anyone, but he deserved what he got as far as I'm concerned. Let sleeping dogs lie."

"Anybody close to the family I could talk with?"

She refilled the wine glasses. "Patrick Dowling used to work for a builder called Denis Creen. He's an old man now, but he's all there. He lives about a mile outside the village. I can give you directions, but it's easier to get there on foot by the canal."

Jane was getting tipsy. I suggested she lie down for an hour or two. "I love what you did to Kenny, Jack," she slurred as I carried her to her room. "Beat the living bollix out of him. He had you kicked out of the cops for that. I love a man who fights for his mott, except you didn't win her back. But you were the real winner, even if you don't know it. Motts like her deserve scumbags like him."

As if I needed remining, it was personal between Kenny and me. He'd do everything in his power to have me locked up. Time was not on my side. I put Jane to bed and set out to find Denis Creen on foot.

I needed to clear my head, so I walked by the canal to the house. It took about thirty minutes. The house stood on its own overlooking the canal. It had a glass porch facing the water, built on a base of red bricks. An old man sat in the porch and returned my wave. I walked up the pathway and he beckoned me to come inside. I guessed he was glad of the company.

I made small talk about other things before getting down to the real reason for the visit. The weather is always topical and we chatted about that. Then I told him about my investigation of the murder of Colleen Murphy, a local. He was happy to help in any way possible.

"Paddy Dowling, the father, well, it's not right to talk of the dead, but he gave his wife a terrible time. Drank every penny he earned. Often Bridie, that was his wife, often she'd come up to me of a Friday to get his wages before he could drink them. It was that sort of country back then. Women nowadays wouldn't put up with it, and they're right. Fair's fair."

"Can you tell me about Colleen?"

"Bridie got pregnant, but he didn't change his ways. Some men do not listen, or learn. A week before she was due she went away. I thought she'd left him, and I was happy for her. A couple of weeks later she came back with a new infant, Colleen. Wives didn't leave their husbands back then, unlike today."

"Where did she have the child?"

"Can't say and she did not volunteer information."

Deep in thought, I walked back along the canal, with dusk falling quickly. That straw I was clutching at was starting to grow into an idea. It was growing stronger with every step I took. The prospect of a term in jail made me think that bit harder than usual. Maybe I'd solved the puzzle.

Jane had not recovered from the wine and was still in bed when I returned. Mrs Nagle offered me a nightcap. We sat at a turf-burning cooker in her kitchen. She talked about how hard it was to make a living from a B&B. They used to be the backbone of the tourist industry but a glut of hotels and loss-leading rates had closed many down. She'd continued because it was the only life she knew, and because she had made many friends.

"Does the village have a resident doctor?"

"Not any more. The nearest one is five miles away."

"Was there one here when Colleen Dowling was a child?"

"Yes, a wonderful doctor, Hilary Quirke. She was the salt of the earth, a community doctor. It didn't matter to her whether a patient had money or not. She treated everyone the same. Of course she's retired now."

"Any idea where she lives?"

She had an old biscuit box on the dresser in the kitchen, made of tin. She took it down. The box was filled with all sorts of cards, Christmas cards, thank-you cards, and booking cards. She pulled out one with a robin and snow. It was a recent Christmas card.

"Her address is on the card."

We stayed the night and started out early next morning. I dropped Jane off, and made a call to Dermot Brady. He informed me that my file had been sent to the Director of Public Prosecutions. Kenny was pushing for a trial.

In the afternoon I phoned Amy Reddy and made an apology. She was gracious enough to accept it without reservation. There was no need to tell her I'd acted like a fool. She agreed to meet me later for a drink. I promised to be on my best behaviour.

A murder case is like a pile of bricks lying on the ground. They look like nothing until you start to build with them. Then they form into a building you begin to recognise. They take shape and you see the final result. That's how it had been with this case. All I needed now was the final proof.

I'd figured out Barry Allen's part in the whole scheme of things too. He'd been suffering from the worst disease known to man or woman. It's called jealousy, or the green-eyed monster. That's why he'd ordered his goon to beat me up. He'd seen me as a rival for Amy's affections. She was the eye candy he needed to parade before the voters. She had class, and he had none. Class is the only commodity that can't be bought off the shelf. Allen must have figured with Amy at his side that people would forget he was a crook. He should have known they'd already forgotten. The Irish have worse memories than dyslexic goldfish.

"Chocolates, Jack?"

"I can't afford a Rolls Royce."

We met in the Gresham Hotel, where I'd made a total fool of myself and ruined her night. I needed to regain her trust. She had a gin, and I limited my intake to a single pint. I should have been eating humble pie, but they didn't serve that.

"How is the investigation going, Jack?"

"Think I've solved it."

"Are you thinking of becoming a real detective?"

She said it in jest, with a grin. Murder was a long way from what I usually did, insurance scams. My future had been on the line. That prospect had concentrated my mind. What I needed to do was find the woman who'd posed as Colleen Murphy. I had a good idea where to find her.

"Thought for a while you'd set me up, Amy."

"Me? Why?"

"Well, I asked myself what you saw in me."

"Ever hear of beauty and the beast?"

"I never said you were a beast, Amy."

My phone interrupted the conversation. Brady came on to tell me that they were proceeding with the case against the number one suspect, who just happened to be me. The public were unhappy with the slow progress, and there was an election coming up. Two people were dead and nobody had been charged. Important people were piling on the pressure too.

We said goodnight outside the hotel and I promised to call her soon. For a few hours afterwards I just stretched out on the sofa and ran the case over in my mind, again and again. I had all the answers, except one. Why had she set me up? I couldn't get my head around that one. It kept me awake until dawn shed its first light over the city.

CHAPTER FIFTEEN

Jane's face could be read easier than a cheap novel. Her head jerked in the direction of my office. Then she gave me the full lowdown on the person waiting for me there. She said it was a person I should not see. She wasn't chewing gum or doing her nails, so it had to be serious. She was right, of course. It was the only person in the world I didn't wish to see.

"Hello, Jack."

"Patricia."

A man can draw a line under the past, but it does not go away. It's there, awaiting a trigger to set it off. Somebody wise said that the past is a different country. Somebody should invent a cure for the past to make a man forget. There should be a pill to wipe out memories. They already had a pill to wipe out a headache.

"Jack, you're looking well."

"Still taking my looking-well pills."

There was that strained awkward silence between us that always happens between a man and a woman who've broken up. There is an uneasy truce between them. The conversation is never flowing or spontaneous. A joke didn't seem appropriate either. We'd been too close, much too close.

"I heard you're in trouble."

"Nothing I can't take care of."

"Is my husband involved?"

"Let's just say I'm not his favourite person."

To break down the barriers I asked if she had kids. She had three, and showed me their pictures on her phone. She was proud of them. I think most mothers are proud of their kids. She put the phone back in her handbag.

"I didn't mean to hurt you, Jack."

"It's called life. This a social visit?"

"You didn't marry?"

"This a social visit?"

Her head shook in the same way as before. I recalled the way she used to hesitate and fidget. Small things a man can't forget. She clasped and unclasped the bag in the same way as before. I went to the window and lit up. A cool gush of air entered the room. It couldn't blow away the tension. I tried to close it, but it stuck. Another job the landlord should have done. It took several attempts before the wind stopped blowing.

"They're bad for your health, Jack. You've become thin."

"Maybe that's why everybody is getting more obese, because smoking is banned everywhere. Ever think of that? Too much fucken political correction in this country for my liking. Anyway, it's my business, not yours."

The desk phone rang and I picked it up.

"Want me to get you out of there?" Jane asked.

"No, it's okay."

Across the river I saw workmen entering the unfinished building that had been earmarked for a bank. There'd been talk everywhere of the economy picking up again. Maybe it was, but the politicians were certain to screw it up again. They'd bribe the voters again with public money. Anything for power. I walked back to my desk. She hadn't changed at all.

"I need someone I can trust. It's my husband…"

She didn't mention him by name. I put two and two together, and came up with four. I recognised the look on her face. She was too embarrassed to talk, so I had to talk for her. I also had to supply a handkerchief for her eyes. That's a woman's greatest asset, her tears.

"Let me guess, he's playing the field and you want me to prove he's playing the field?"

"Something of that nature, yes. Why is he doing it?"

"With most men it's called a middle-age crisis. With him I suspect it's something else. I don't think you'll like what I have to say. I don't wish to hurt you, and words do hurt. I'm too old now for platitudes."

"Go on, Jack, I can take it."

"You married him when he was an ambitious cop. Now he's a superintendent, and if he can solve this case by framing me he'll get the Commissioner's job. He'll be moving in the top circle of society, mixing with judges and ambassadors, and the people who matter in our society. He'll need a new shirt seven days a week, and acting lessons. He thinks you're not good enough for him now he's on his way to the top. So he's on the lookout for someone younger and single."

"What do you think?"

"Me? I'm not your husband."

That's how it goes. She'd been attracted to him by his naked ambition, but now it was driving them apart. It wasn't her fault. A woman has not only to think for herself but also for any kids she might have. She'd compared Kenny to me, and chosen him.

It happened all the time.

"What sort of evidence do you require?"

"I don't understand, Jack."

"Don't ask me to spell it out."

"Oh, I see now. Everything."

There was a strange irony to this assignment. Kenny was out to nail me, and I was out to nail him. I had no qualms about taking the case. Kenny was prepared to jail an innocent man to further his career. I was now out to wreck that career. He had no place in a modern police force.

*

Before driving up the Wicklow Mountains. I wheeled into the Internet café on the quays and had a cup of coffee and a bun. I could surf the Internet on my own by now, without the help of the waitress. It confirmed my hunch, but I needed more advice from an expert. Then the car headed out of the city and up the mountains.

I had the address of Doctor Hilary Quirke, but I couldn't find the house. There were no signposts for miles, and the weather was coming down. The country roads were deserted of traffic, with no ramblers in sight. After an hour of searching I spotted a man out walking his dog who gave me directions.

Ten minutes later I was parked near a gateway with a pillar on each side and a stone lion on each pillar. Now it was a question of waiting. I didn't know if it would take a day or a month. I was prepared to wait for as long as it took.

If asked to define my line of work, I'd have to say waiting.

I think Samuel Beckett wrote a play about it. Waiting outside a house for the occupant to come out, the same occupant that was supposed to be in bed with a broken back. Except he hadn't got a broken back but was scamming the insurance company.

Waiting outside the home of a woman suing Dublin Corporation for the loss of her sex life after tripping over a pavement stone. Except she picked up men at clubs and brought them home to her bed. Some people think it's a victimless crime, scamming an insurance company. They're wrong. Every crime has a victim.

I spent the whole day near the entrance, drinking tea from a flask and eating sandwiches. Darkness drifted quickly over the mountains and settled on the parked car. She hadn't shown. I packed it in at seven that night and headed back to the lighted city. It proved to be the first weekend of many.

Joe Kelly and I had attended the same school, but after that our paths had diverged. His career had gone north, and mine had gone south. He was now a top surgeon in the Mater Hospital on the north side of the city. Jane found him on the phone and put me through. Appealing to our friendship at school, I asked for a favour. He listened as I briefly outlined my problem. I related what Alan Jones had told me about identical twins.

"He's retired about fifteen years, Jack. Probably switched off from medical advances. Up to very recently both scientists and doctors believed monozygotic twins were identical. It was not questioned because it was accepted as scientific fact. Then it was discovered that there was a difference in human DNA sequencing. It was so minute that it had been overlooked before, and was only found with the aid of the latest medical instruments."

"Identical twins are not identical?"

"No, but it takes a real expert to spot the difference. Furthermore, that expert has to know what he or she is looking for. The difference is so tiny that it can be easily overlooked. Are you thinking of taking up a real job?"

"No, I'd rather eat chips than caviar. Listen, Joe, I have two lab reports giving the same result. One sample is from a deceased woman, and another is from a live woman. How can that sort of thing happen?"

"Cross contamination maybe."

"That's been ruled out. What else?"

"Never rule out human nature. When people examine results and find comparison after comparison the same, they tend to switch off. It happens in every profession. The brain often makes its own assumptions and takes shortcuts. Why do you think airline pilots and co-pilots use check lists?"

"I thought we were discussing identical twins, Joe?"

"If you listen I'll tell you how confusion happens. The airline industry had many crashes because the brains of pilots were taking shortcuts. The problem was solved by the introduction of check lists. Now pilots must go through them before taking off. They have introduced check lists in many American hospitals too in order to cut down human error. It's obvious to me that the people who examined both DNA files jumped to the conclusion that they were the same. To put it another way, they didn't know what they were looking for."

"But they're supposed to be experts, Joe."

"First, they are human, Jack. Take it from me, no two persons are the same. I'll stake my considerable reputation on that call. I'll send you my bill later."

That last remark was his idea of a joke.

I hired a car to follow Kenny. He was familiar with my car so I didn't want to scare him off. It was a small Mazda silver in colour, with no outstanding features. It looked much the same as any other car on the road. He lived in Lucan, a suburb of the city on the south side. It was a large house set on its own plot, with a wall surrounding the rear. If I saw him emerging in his uniform, I abandoned the tail. That light blue uniform was too conspicuous. People tended to remember a uniform. There were two cars parked in front of the house, a saloon and a people carrier. I spotted Patricia driving the people carrier to school a couple of times with kids in the back. I didn't think she saw me because the newspaper covered my face as she drove past. I was waiting again.

In mid-week Kenny exited the house dressed in civvies and got into the saloon. Patricia had driven out earlier. He drove a Nissan, white in colour, with Dublin plates. I let him pass, and followed. He turned towards the city.

The woman was blonde and old enough to sleep with, but young enough to replace his wife. She must have known he was married, even if he'd removed his wedding ring somewhere on the journey. Kenny appeared on TV regularly as a spokesman for the cops, the sort of exposure that furthered his career and ambition. I could see his naked finger in the mirror in the bar of the hotel. They were seated at a table having lunch and I was seated at the bar reading a newspaper. I had a glass in front of me filled with red lemonade, but it looked like a large whiskey to the casual observer.

My phone snapped them in the mirror a few times, but I needed more. Meeting a woman in the hotel for a meal could easily have been explained away. He might have explained that she was a witness in a trial and he'd been gathering some information. He might have explained that she was a work colleague, or a supplier of stationery to the force. I needed better evidence, the sort of evidence they were there to perform. A cleaning lady walked past with a vacuum cleaner in tow and I followed her.

Next morning I asked Jane to phone Patricia with a message that the parcel had arrived. It was a code we'd arranged. It meant I had the necessary evidence. Then I asked Jane to have the pictures downloaded from the phone. There was a shop on the quays that specialised in that sort of thing. I needed hard copies to give to her. After that, I told Jane to delete the images from the phone.

She arrived in the afternoon, feeling a reason to explain that she'd left the kids with her mother. I had the pictures in a large envelope, and pushed them across the desk. I left her there to study them and chatted with Jane. She'd decided to move in with her boyfriend. Talk of marriage was in the air, but that was long off in the future.

"What's he do?"

"He's a graphic designer."

"Not a celebrity?"

"I've had it up to my neck with them bastards."

Patricia had been crying. She composed herself when I returned to the office. I think she'd known all along. She just required the final proof. A confirmation of her fears.

"I'm sorry if the pictures offend you."

"How did you get these?"

"Bribed a cleaner. She took them."

She turned them over and over, as if trying to convince herself that the man in the bed wasn't her husband. She wanted it to be him, and she didn't want it to be him. Now she had to make a decision. She couldn't simply walk away. She had kids, and he was their father.

"Who is the woman?"

"Don't know. Does it matter?"

She didn't answer. I was about to tell her that her husband was a serial cheater, but kept my mouth buttoned. I had no hard evidence except a gut feeling. It was a time for silence. She asked how much for the service. I told her Jane handled the accounts.

Before she left, I offered some advice.

"He'll deny the undeniable, Patricia. He'll wriggle like a worm on a hook to get off. He's aiming for the top job and that means thinking like a politician. I can't tell you what to do, but the evidence you have there is a powerful tool. He can't afford to let that into the public domain. It'll ruin his prospects of getting the top job. That's all he cares about."

"Not me or the kids?"

"He's a *mefeiner,* we both know that."

I didn't have to tell her much more. Sure, Kenny cared for her, but she was third in line. His kids were second in line. That top job was head of his priorities. That's what he wanted most of all, and he was on his way.

"Thanks for your help."

"Any time. Let me know what you do."

She didn't get in touch with me after that. Maybe she was too ashamed, though she had nothing to be ashamed about. I heard afterwards that she'd divorced

Kenny and moved away. They had obviously come to an agreement. I don't know where she went, whether she stayed at home or emigrated. Whatever deal she'd made, Kenny remained in his job.

The waiting continued near the home of Doctor Hilary Quirke at the weekends. I'd made inquiries about the doctor around the locality. She lived with her husband, a retired engineer, in the house up the mountains. They were a quiet couple, occasionally walking and playing golf. They were well respected by everyone I spoke to. The husband wasn't in good health and had to be escorted when going to the golf club. They had three children, a son and two daughters. All three had emigrated, but one daughter had recently been seen at the house. She matched the description of the mystery woman.

Business was starting to pick up, although the insurance companies were giving me a wide berth. The whiff of murder still clung to me like a rotten fish. Brady was keeping me on the inside track, telling me what was going down. He put his job on the line for me. I owed him big time, so I invited him out for lunch. It was the least I could do.

"The jigsaw is nearly complete, except for one piece."

"Why the hell can't you tell me, Jack?"

"Because I might be wrong, that's why."

We were in a hotel twenty miles south of the capital, an out-of-the-way place. Brady was keeping a low profile. Kenny was on the warpath. He'd discovered I had supplied the evidence for the divorce. Patricia had probably told him. Now he had a better incentive to nail me, not that he needed one.

"He hasn't forgiven you for beating him up either."

"He has a pension for life, I don't."

"Sometimes satisfaction beats a pension hands down."

We choked on our hot meal over that crack. Brady had been present at the fight. Nobody had stepped in to stop it. I had won the fight, and lost my job. That's usually the way. There are seldom outright winners in anything.

CHAPTER SIXTEEN

The waiting finally paid off. I saw her again, and she was alive. She walked up a mountain track between two elderly people. I hadn't seen the elderly couple before, but I suspected they were Doctor Hilary Quirke and her husband. He was unsteady on his feet, aided by the two women holding his arms. Their backs were turned, so I couldn't see her face. But the walk was unmistakable.

She had the walk of a big African cat, light and springy on her feet. I remembered how she'd walked up the stairs on the night she'd murdered Paul Murphy. It was the same walk, and no two people walk the same.

They entered between the pillars and walked up to the house. Figuring she'd recognise the number plates, I slipped on a pair of false ones, securing them with rubber bands. The waiting now started in earnest.

She drove a Citroen with French plates and wore stylish clothes. She had a little girl in the car, aged about ten. The VW followed, and I acted like a casual driver on a day out. She slowed down to a crawl to let me pass. That was the last thing I wanted, but I had to pass. I relied on a cap to conceal my identity, and drove fast. But I got the plate number of the Citroen. I made a call to Dermot Brady and gave him the number.

"I work in Dublin, Jack, not Paris."

"Use your contacts and your discretion."

"Get offside now. This is a job for the professionals."

"No, I have to finish it myself."

"I'll give you a week. After that I'm taking over."

On Sunday morning I drove between the pillars with the lions on top and up a winding gravel track to the house. It had red ivy growing on the façade and a dozen widows on both floors. The door had a fanlight and was painted green. It had no buzzer, but a large brass knocker announced my arrival. An elderly woman opened the door with grey hair tied in a bun and rimless spectacles.

I handed her my card and enquired if she minded answering a few questions. She seemed surprised by my visit.

"A private detective? Why should you want to question me?"

"It's about your daughter."

"I have two daughters."

"It's about the daughter of the late Brigid Dowling."

The name registered on her face. She was caught in two minds. She could protect her adopted daughter by turning me away, or she could come to terms what that daughter had done. The door opened wide.

"You had better come in."

She explained that her husband suffered from Alzheimer's disease. Nothing made sense to him, except the past. He lived in the past, not the present. Some people want to forget the past. He couldn't escape from it. It was a progressive disease, with no known cure.

"We had a good life."

"At least you were left with memories, missus."

"I'm thankful because my husband has none."

He sat on a sofa in the living room watching ads on TV. He'd been a big man in his youth, judging from his frame. I don't think he knew I was there. The doctor offered tea but I declined. It was not a time for the social taking of tea or polite conversation. It was finally a time for answers.

"What's your daughter's name?"

"I have two daughters, Mister Russell."

"Your adopted daughter?"

"Carol. How much have you found out?"

"Mostly everything."

"That Colleen Murphy was her twin?"

"Yes, her identical twin."

She had a guilt complex, although she didn't have to. She'd acted in the best interests of the mother and the baby. An act of charity thirty-five years ago between a doctor and her patient. Brigid Dowling could not have reared twins, not with her feckless husband. Hilary Quirke had taken one twin as her own child. She hadn't formally adopted the baby because then everyone would have known, including the father. Brigid Dowling had returned home with one baby, and nobody knew she'd given birth to twins.

One had grown up in a household that struggled to survive, and one had grown up in a household with no money worries. But the real damage had nothing to do with money. The real damage had been done by splitting up the twins.

"I broke all medical protocols, Mr Russell."

"For the right reasons."

"Sometimes that's not good enough."

"You weren't to know the future. Nobody can see that far."

"They were hard times," she began. "I knew women back then who didn't know what their husbands earned. We've changed a lot since then, and all for the better. Brigid and I made a pact to keep the matter to ourselves, not even telling the twins. My other two, Sean and Deirdre, accepted Carol as their sister. But for some reason, she didn't accept them. She instinctively knew that they were not related by blood."

"I guess she felt incomplete without her twin."

"Yes, I believe that is true, Mr Russell. She didn't accept them because she was closer to her twin. She knew deep inside that she had a twin. I've been reading up on identical twins. It's uncanny how close they can be. No scientist has come close to understanding how special the bond is."

"I'm beginning to understand it myself," I replied.

"We didn't know any better in those days."

Her act of charity had separated two sisters who should have grown up in the same household. Every action, good or bad, has its own unforeseen and unintended consequence. But nobody can see into the future. She didn't have a crystal ball back then. She couldn't have seen that her act of kindness would lead to the death of Paul Murphy.

"Carol used to wake up at night calling out for her sister, and she wasn't calling for Deirdre. I recall one occasion when she had all the symptoms of measles, although she wasn't sick. Afterwards I discovered that Colleen had measles, at precisely the same time that her twin fell ill. They felt each other's pain."

"Where does she live now?"

"In France, in the south."

"She was a dancer growing up?"

"No, a gymnast. Quite good too."

"Did she do it professionally?"

No, for leisure. She's a qualified chemist with a string of shops. Well, she did have a string of shops but sold them off last year. She has a daughter and lives for her. She's sending her to a private school in Switzerland."

"The same private school you sent her to?"

"Yes, I believed in giving her a good start in life."

"When was she home last?"

"In December. She's thinking of returning to live here. I think it's a spiritual thing, to be closer to the memory of her twin. Colleen should have been buried. That way she would have had a grave to visit.

Why was Colleen cremated?"

"To remove any evidence. Her husband murdered her."

Her lack of reaction suggested she already knew. She knew what the dogs in the street had known for a long time. Murphy had killed his wife. He might have gotten away with the murder too because he had connections in the right places. The case never came to court because a bullet had intervened.

"And you believe Carol took revenge?" she asked.

"Seems that way, yes."

"She was reared to be forgiving, Mr Russell."

"Not when it came to the murder of her twin."

Perhaps she felt responsible somehow for the death of Murphy. The doctor had reared her to distinguish right from wrong. But a stronger and more powerful feeling had taken control. I was finding out that no stronger feeling existed in the world. Not the love between a man and a woman, or the love between other siblings. Nothing came as close.

"What will happen now?"

"She'll be arrested. The law is a game of chance, but she can plead mitigating circumstances. She has a little girl. That should count too. Perhaps she has a mental condition…"

"No, Mr Russell, she is quite sane."

"Temporary insanity is still an option."

"Her child might be taken into custody if that happened. Of course I would try to obtain custody, but I have my husband to look after. He requires constant attention as you can see. The courts might take her child away."

Changing my mind, I asked for tea. My hands had nothing to do. Also, I needed something tangible to feel more comfortable. She made tea in a china pot with patterns of red roses. It was a nice house, and she was a good woman. However, not her or any force under the sun could have stopped Carol. Once her twin was killed, Paul Murphy had to die. He had murdered part of Carol too.

That wouldn't count in court, of course, if she went on trial. The jury would see a live woman standing in the dock, not realising half of her was dead.

"When did you tell her about Colleen?"

"On her tenth birthday. She said it was the best present she ever received. They began writing to each other. We took Colleen on holidays with us a few times and the two were inseparable. They even slept in the same bed."

She stopped talking, as if unwilling to go on. The memories were still raw. She sipped the tea slowly. A large clock on the wall ticked down the seconds. Perhaps taking about the past helped her come to terms with the present.

"The worst part was separating them again after their holidays together. We literally had to tear them apart. Carol used to cry herself to sleep for weeks on end. Do you have any idea what that does to a mother?"

"Why didn't she attend Colleen's wedding?"

"The twins lived in their own private world, and I

think Carol wanted it to remain that way. Time does not allow things to remain as they are, does it? Paul Murphy did not know of Carol's existence because she wanted it that way. That's why she didn't act as the bridesmaid. Sarah Corbally didn't know either. She fulfilled the role of bridesmaid in the belief that Colleen was an only child. Do you understand?"

"I do now. They lived in their own world."

Carol had killed Paul Murphy as an act of revenge. She had applied the ancient law of an eye for an eye. Murphy had also killed half of Carol too when he'd murdered her twin sister. He had signed his own death warrant by killing Colleen. I had all the answers, except one. I couldn't figure out why she'd framed me. I had to hear that from her own lips.

"Do you wish to stay for dinner, Mr Russell?"

"Thanks, but I have to get back."

"We're expecting Carol."

"Okay, I'll stay for lunch."

She didn't have to tell me Carol was coming to dinner. She could have kept dumb and warned Carol. I guessed she believed in doing the right thing. Perhaps she was trying to correct the mistakes of the past. The past is indeed a foreign country. They do things differently there.

I went outside and lit up. White mists covered the mountains in wispy garments. The trees were taking on leaves again. Spring was in the air. I moved the car to the side of the house, out of view. That way Carol wouldn't take fright and drive off before I could talk with her. Then I called Brady.

"I'm on my way. Stall her."

"Right, don't take too long."

"The sooner she's under lock and key the better."

"She isn't dangerous."

"No? Tell that to Paul Murphy."

The doctor prepared dinner in the kitchen – a leg of lamb. She seasoned it with thyme and put it in the oven. She'd been a good mother to Carol, but nobody can replace a natural mother. The law of unintended consequences.

"Want a hand, doctor?"

"Yes, you can wash the potatoes."

The Citroen pulled into the driveway at noon. She emerged with a little girl. Her appearance had changed radically. Her hair was cropped and dyed blonde. She had a healthy tan, bronzed and toned. The little girl had brown hair and blue eyes. She wore a red pinafore dress with white fringes. She had the strong features of her mother.

"Hello, Colleen."

"How do you know my name?" the little girl asked.

"A lucky guess. Hello Carol."

"I'm sorry, but we haven't met."

My presence in the house hadn't thrown her. She acted as if we'd never met. I said we needed to talk outside the house, not in the presence of the doctor and the child. She weighed it up, and agreed. She told the little girl to enter the house.

We walked down the driveway a bit. I dropped a

cigarette and stopped to pick it up. I watched her walk. It was slinky and smooth. It was the same walk I'd seen on the night she'd killed Paul Murphy, a feline walk. She was in good shape.

"You almost got away with it, Carol."

"Whatever do you mean?"

"The planning, the research. But you made a mistake with the phial containing the DNA samples. You left a print on that, and the cops have it. They can lock you up on that evidence."

Sure, I was throwing her a line. There were no fingerprints on the phial. My fingerprints were on the phial. I knew that, but she didn't. She had planned the murder well, but I had sown a doubt in her mind. It was a game of bluff. She didn't look at me but through me, like an actor playing a part. I told her that a detective was on the way. She kept her cool. I reckoned the loss of her twin had hardened her to any condition life could throw her way. Nothing could faze her after losing the person closest to her.

"What are you selling, Mr Russell?"

"Freedom. Either yours, or mine."

So she began to talk, trying to discover how much I knew. I informed her that I had all the facts, except one. Why had she framed me? That was the missing piece of the jigsaw. All the other pieces had fallen into place except that single piece. I reminded her that a detective was on the way. She could talk with him, or talk with me. She was clever. Anyone who could have planned the murder of Paul Murphy in such a manner had to be clever.

"Are you wired, Jack?"

"I was, until you robbed the device. It cost me a fortune too. Not to mention my mobile phone. I know you destroyed it because it didn't ping when you left that night. That phone cost me a hundred euro and it wasn't insured."

"Take off your shirt."

I glanced back at the house, about fifty metres away. Its view was obscured by a curvature in the driveway. We were out of sight. I recall cobwebs on the hedge laden with white dew. They resembled works of art.

"What about paying me first?"

"You'll only put it on a horse. Take the shirt off."

I undressed in the driveway, taking off layers of clothes, down to the shirt. Then I unbuttoned the shirt and pulled up my vest. She walked around me to satisfy herself I wasn't wired. She was satisfied with the result.

"The keys to the house that night you murdered him? It had me puzzled how you'd gotten your hands on them. Most people keep keys hidden outside in case they lock themselves out. Your twin was one of those people, and that's how you knew where to find them."

I reckoned she'd gotten the props on the Internet, the make-up to look dead and the fake bullet hole. She'd hired a private detective to track my movements. That's how she'd known all about my movements and Jane's break times. That's how she'd kept track of me. The planning had been faultless.

"Private eyes are competitors, Carol, but we do co-operate. Basically, we're on the side of law and order. Tom Dalton told me everything. He can identify you too, by the way."

"His word against mine, Jack."

"It all adds up in the end. It's the same as building a wall with a pile of single bricks. Brick by brick, it builds up. His evidence, my evidence, the prints, the motive. Paul Murphy murdered your twin sister, and you murdered him. An eye for an eye."

"Maybe he deserved to die, Jack."

"That wasn't your decision."

"No? Whose decision was it then?"

"The law."

"Whose law is that, Jack? The law for the poor, or the law for the rich? No need to answer that, is there? The evidence speaks for itself. But you were building a case against me. Do continue."

"Thirty-five years ago, in a small village in a rural part of the country, a woman fell pregnant. That woman was your mother, Mrs Brigid Dowling. Except she was married to a man who supported the pub instead of her. Sometimes she had to visit his employer to get the wages before he got his hands on the money. When your mother went to the doctor she was told to expect twins. That doctor was Hilary Quirke, who took you home as her own. It was an act of mercy because your mother couldn't support two babies, not with a feckless husband. A lot of husbands were in those days. Nobody knew about the arrangement except your mother and Hilary Quirke and her husband. How am I doing so far?"

"I'm still listening."

"But there's a special bond between identical twins that nobody can explain, not even doctors or scientists. They seem to think the same and read each other's thoughts. Some can't bear to be separated, not even to get married. Somehow Colleen and you knew there was something missing, that neither of you was complete. The doctor finally confirmed that you had a twin and you were joined again. That's how you knew so much about Colleen's lifestyle, her friends, the layout of the house, and the fact that her husband wasn't a knight in shining armour."

"What man is, Jack?"

"Sir Galahad."

I think that brought a smile to her face, but I'm not sure. I think she could hide her emotions whenever she felt under threat from the world. I'd have hated to play poker against her. That's a game where you need to keep your emotions hidden. It's not a game for people of a nervous disposition.

"My misjudgement, Jack. I thought you were dumb."

"Only the bookies are allowed to think that."

"Of course, the horses. Gambling is a sign of weakness."

Maybe she was right. I'd always considered it a hobby. It certainly didn't pay the rent. She had no weaknesses, that much was obvious. She had nerves of steel.

"I always knew part of me was missing, Jack. It was as if half of me was somewhere else. After I found out about Colleen, I felt whole again. We communicated daily, by phone, by letter, even when I was sent to boarding school on the continent. We holidayed together. There is no feeling in the world better than being with someone who can read your thoughts."

"She told you she was planning to divorce Murphy. That much I figured out. I think she also realised he couldn't bear the thought of giving her half of everything. He'd rather kill her instead. She tell you he was going to kill her?"

"She didn't have to because I could read her thoughts. When he did kill her, I felt the bullet." She pointed to the same spot she'd shown me on her first visit. "Here, Jack. I felt her pain, and her despair. She died and I lived. I wanted to die for a month or two, but I have a daughter."

"So you did the next best thing? Revenge?"

"There is no sweeter fruit. I killed him and I sleep good at night. No conscience, or no regrets. Do you think the State would have convicted her killer, Jack? A rich man? A member of the Law Society?"

She had a good point. The State had a poor record when dealing with the rich and famous. Paul Murphy had been rich and he had been famous. He had also been part of the legal system, a pillar of the establishment. The chances of him ever going to jail for murder had been less than a snowball's chances of survival in the Sahara Desert at noon. That's why she'd taken the law into her own hands. Murder can't be condoned, but I did understand her motive.

"Remember I asked you about the green dress

supplied by Darren Pringle? That question threw you because you didn't know about that dress. Colleen hadn't told you because it was Christmas and she had other things on her mind. You told me you were shot whilst wearing that dress, but Colleen was wearing her wedding dress."

"You figured that out all by yourself? And you're the man who can't back a winner for skins?"

Gambling was a hobby, but solving the crime had been more important. Losing on a horse might ruin my day, but not solving the crime would have ruined my future. That's why I'd lost sleep at nights running it over and over again in my head. The prospect of losing my freedom had made me think harder.

"I've figured out more things too. How did the cops turn up at the house that night so soon after the killing? Nobody could have heard the gunshot. Besides, there were fireworks making similar noises. You made a phone call to the cops telling them about the gunshot. That call didn't come from your mobile phone but from a kiosk. There's one about a mile from the house. Calls from a kiosk can't be traced."

"My, my, I am impressed."

Perhaps she'd worn her wedding dress that night as an ironic symbol to remind him of his marriage vows. It hadn't worked. There's no mention of money in marriage vows. Perhaps there should be. But that might spoil the romance.

"One question, Carol. Why me?"

"You're the one with all the answers, Jack."

"Your father was a loser. You blamed him for the

splitting you from your sister. You have a daughter, but no mention of her father. It's my guess you used him and then dumped him because no man could ever replace your sister. How am I doing?"

"So far so good."

"Men are not your favourite species, are they, Carol? So when you were looking for a sacrificial goat, it had to be a man. I happen to be a man. But why me?"

"Nothing personal, Jack, I just needed the right man for the frame. You were that man. A former cop thrown out of the force for violent conduct over a woman. A man with a name and a temper to match. And when you beat up Paul Murphy, that was the icing on the cake. I could not have planned it better myself. I bet you felt good after giving him that hiding."

"I'm glad it wasn't personal. I'd hate to see what you'd do if it was personal."

"Try to see this from my perspective. I framed you, but I didn't kill you. It would not have been difficult to kill Murphy and his partner, and then kill you. A classic murder-suicide. End of story, end of investigation."

"Maybe I should be grateful for small mercies."

"I'm not a mindless killer, Jack."

She was wearing a long tweed coat and both her hands were planted in the pockets. I knew why when a gun appeared in her right hand. It was made of metal, and I suspected it wasn't a toy. There was no doubt in my mind that she could shoot straight. She had proved that once. I didn't need her to prove it twice.

CHAPTER SEVENTEEN

Colleen Murphy had told her twin about the Mauser, and where to locate it in the house. She'd used that gun to kill Paul Murphy. I can't say where she got the second gun, except that it was aimed at my heart. It was a revolver with a small snout, just the right size for a pocket.

"Don't be stupid, Carol. I'm not your enemy."

"Ah, but you are, Jack. Paul Murphy took my sister away. Now he's dead. Another man wants to separate me from my daughter. She's the only reminder I have of her. When I look into her eyes, I see my twin again."

"Your sister is dead, Carol. Your daughter is a human being in her own right. She is not a reincarnation of your sister. Think of her before doing anything stupid."

"I am, Jack. Nobody is going to separate us."

The trauma of separation was still raw with her. She had not recovered from the parting. I knew nobody could separate her now from her daughter. She was the only remaining link to her dead twin. And that made Carol very dangerous. She would kill to protect her daughter. She ordered me to hand over my phone, and the gun said I couldn't refuse.

"We're going for a drive, Jack."

"What about dinner? It's a long time since I had lamb."

She threw me a bunch of keys, telling me to drive the Citroen. I could smell the leather in the car and the lamb cooking in the kitchen. I looked up at the sky before closing the car door. It was grey and overcast, but it was still not a good day to die.

"Listen, Carol, a judge might give you a light sentence for killing Paul Murphy. A temporary rush of blood, the closeness to your identical twin, that sort of thing. But this is different. This is pre-meditated, and they give you life for that."

"I don't intend to kill you, Jack. After all, I could not have avenged my sister without your help. You were the fall guy and performed that role well. Now, let's go for a drive."

"So what are we doing? Wicklow is a lovely county, but not in this weather. We should come back in the summer."

I was not her twin. I could not read her mind. Maybe she did intend to kill me, maybe not. But her gun was giving orders and I had to obey. It indicated that we turn left after we exited between the pillars. The only thing I could do was play for time, and pray that Brady would turn up soon. Time was not on my side, and I had to play for it like a gambler. My bad luck had to change sooner or later.

"Jane drove me down. She knows I'm here too."

"On Sunday? Men make such bad liars. Besides, I

saw your car at the side of the house. Relax, Jack. Talk to me about your brother. Why don't you keep in touch?"

Her research was good. I did have a brother and a couple of nieces and nephews. We saw each other at Christmas. Once a year was good enough for me. Christmases spent with family always lead to rows. The season of goodwill usually ends in tears. The Christmas dinner at his house a couple of years back had almost ended in a fist fight.

"We're not close."

"Then you don't know how it feels, do you?"

"We're brothers, not identical twins."

The car ascended steadily, driving up the winding road with mountains on one side and valleys on the other. I recognised the road. I'd been here before with Amy Reddy. It was the road to Glendalough. I thought about Amy briefly, and whether I'd see her again. She hadn't been part of the conspiracy against me. She had been straight with me down the line.

"Do you think I'm crazy, Jack?"

"No more than anyone else in this crazy country."

"Because I believe in reincarnation? Some of the world's great religions believe in it too. They can't all be crazy. It's a matter of belief. They can't put me in jail for that."

"Maybe not, but they can for murder."

"I believe my daughter is the reincarnation of my twin."

"Don't tell her that, Carol."

"Why not?"

"Because she'll never forgive you when she grows up. I don't know how this thing is going to end, but I do know that kids must live their own lives. They can't live in the shadows of others because they are individuals in their own right. They must make their own way through life."

"I didn't realise you were a philosopher, Jack."

"I'm not, but I do know about human nature."

We passed a signpost for Glendalough, and within minutes came to the settlement. The gun told me to keep driving. The car kept to the mountain road. I kept my eyes on the rear-view mirror. Brady was taking his time. We passed under a canopy of fir trees with the pale sun peeping through the branches. I had to keep her onside somehow.

"Where's the father of your daughter, Carol?"

"That's a politically incorrect question."

Time, that's what I played for. It's not important until you think about how long there might be left. Then it's the most important thing in the world. The Citroen moved slowly, and I hoped she wouldn't notice, or check the speedometer. Brady was long overdue.

"You know identical twins haven't the same DNA?"

"Yes, but it takes an expert to spot the difference, Jack. Most of the people who work in the labs are not experts. They are nine-to-five people, doing their job for a weekly wage and going home for the weekends. That's why I felt pretty confident about giving you the samples."

She wasn't listening anymore. The plan was in motion like a military operation. I couldn't take the chance that she was telling the truth, that she didn't intend to kill me. I had the germ of another plan in my mind but I needed luck. I was hoping for an oncoming car to swerve into and create confusion. I wasn't having much luck. The winding mountain road was deserted, confirming my run of bad luck.

From behind a drifting cloud, rays of sunshine appeared. The pines we passed were heavy with sap after the rains. The car rolled along at a steady forty kilometres. It was the sort of day you tend to remember, if you can survive it long enough to remember. Somehow the horses didn't seem to matter anymore. More important matters occupied my mind.

We emerged from the pines and drove between hills of furze bushes before the land flattened out. She pointed to a lay-by and told me to pull in. The road was uneven, highs and lows, and covered in potholes. A track wound its way from the road to an old stone house with no windows.

"I forgot my walking shoes too, Carol."

"Still don't trust me, eh?"

"It's called learning from experience."

The track was littered with stones and rubble. I stumbled a few times climbing up to the house. Her feet didn't miss a step. The house had thick concrete walls and grey slates on the roof. The door was solid and had bolts on the outside, rusted with age.

"I used to play up here when I was the same age as

my child, Jack. I used to watch the farmers with their sheepdogs rounding up the sheep. When the snows were bad they used to put the sheep in that old house. It kept them warm and protected them from foxes."

"Looks like a tomb to me."

"You'll only have to spend a couple of days here. That'll give me enough time to get out of the country. I'll phone and let the authorities know where to find you. Let's just say it's my way of making amends."

"I'm supposed to be thankful for my life?"

"Everybody should be, Jack."

Below us, on the road, a car pulled up and parked behind the Citroen. It was Brady's car. He opened the passenger door, keeping the car between us as a shield. He called out that he was armed, and ordered her to drop the gun. The seconds became minutes and the minutes stretched into hours. Everything happened in slow motion. Carol stopped and took aim. I can't say if she intended to shoot or warn him off. Brady wasn't the type to be warned off, even if she'd been holding a bazooka. A shot rang out in the still air. It was a warning shot from Brady. I can't recall if a second shot was fired because I reacted. The little girl needed a mother. Too many people had died already.

The rush knocked her down on the stones and we grappled for the gun. Brady was on the scene in seconds. She fought like a cat but he managed to cuff her. We both bundled her into the rear of his car. After the initial scuffle she quietened down. She was making other plans. She wasn't the type to give in that easily.

"Doctor Quirke said I might find you up here."

"You saw the little girl?"

"Nice kid. Glad I didn't have to shoot her mother. A mother can't be replaced, can she? You drive the car back to the house. I'll take her in and caution her under oath. You okay to drive back? You look pretty shook."

"Sure. She can't be separated from her kid, Dermot."

"That's not my department."

"It'll push her over the edge if she is."

"She should have thought of that before murdering Paul Murphy. She had a choice, he didn't. Leave it now, Jack. The law will take it from here."

"What law is that, Dermot? She shot a member of the Law Society. They take care of their own. That's how it works in this country. We both know that much."

"I didn't hear that remark. Even if I had I would reply that the law is impartial. I work for that impartial law. We are friends, Jack, but I'd have no hesitation in arresting you if required. I hope you understand the principle of the supremacy of the law in a democracy."

"Don't you understand? She can't be separated from her kid."

"Oh, so now you're a psychiatrist was well as a detective? Why don't you put that on your CV as well? Draw a line under this whole affair or I will. Got that?"

He sat into the car. Carol was handcuffed in the

rear. She had not given up the struggle. She sat quietly gazing down at the carpet. Her fight hadn't ended. She wouldn't give up her freedom without a fight. I wondered what her next move might be. Carol was making plans for the future.

"One good result came out of this," Brady said, starting the car. "Kenny will not get that promotion. There must be a God up there somewhere. They say that he works in mysterious ways. See you later."

"Maybe you'll get the job."

"Me?" he grinned. "I'm a cop, not a politician."

Driving to the house, I noticed blood on the seat, and ran over the previous events of the day. Then I felt a sharp pain in my elbow. Maybe a second shot had been fired. It needed to be examined by a doctor.

"Lacerations from falling on rocks," Hilary Quirke said. "Did my daughter do this to you?"

She cleaned the wound with something that stung worse than a nest of wasps. She bandaged me up and told me that it wasn't serious. My good jacket was ruined, however, and I didn't have a suitable replacement. More money.

"No, I fell. Two left feet, you know."

"Carol is gone with the detective?"

"Yes, Carol has been arrested. You'll have to think of something to tell the kid. Can I stay here for a few hours? I'm in no condition to drive. My hands are shaking like a leaf in a gale. I'll have a nap for an hour or two, wind down."

"Of course… I'll do everything possible to help my daughter. She's not my flesh and blood, but I have always treated her as such. She is as close to me as my natural children. She's not to blame for her actions."

That was a matter for the courts, but I didn't tell her that. I used to think everyone was responsible for their own actions. Lying on the couch trying to sleep, I wasn't so sure anymore. I was feeling too bad to sleep. The kid was running around and crying for her mother. Pulling a duvet over my head didn't help either because she kept tugging at me and asking for her mother.

Her granny tried everything to comfort the little girl, without success. Nothing could calm her down. Finally, the heat was off me. There was enough evidence to convict Carol Quirke, or whatever surname she used. Instead of feeling good, I felt bad. That little girl haunted my dreams. That's why I took to drinking at nights, so that I could sleep better. The drinking didn't help. Constant nightmares of a kid running wild down dark alleys screaming for her mother saw to that.

Charlie Bastable was glad of the company. His wife didn't understand him anyway. We drank whiskey in Madigan's pub, where journalists gathered to swop information. They talked a lot about the libel laws, and how they couldn't do their job properly with the threat of litigation hanging over their heads. A newspaper had to be vetted by a dozen lawyers before it could hit the streets. The courts had a tendency to hand down lottery-sized awards against newspapers for libel. They could put a newspaper out of business.

"The foundation stone of a free democracy is a free press," someone said. "We should be able to publish and be damned. We'll print an apology if we get it wrong. That should be enough to satisfy anyone."

"The fuel of this country is money," Charlie said. "And the greediest in this country are politicians. They're the main beneficiaries in libel cases. It's the goose that lays the golden egg. Why kill the goose? You're stupid if you think they'll kill that goose by changing the libel laws."

"The libel laws protect secrecy, Charlie. Secrecy was the principle cause of the Celtic Tiger. Everything was done behind closed doors in the corridors of power. It'll happen again if the libel laws aren't reformed. Can't you see that?"

"Want change? Start a fucken revolution!"

We sat in a corner away from the hubbub. Charlie wore his heart on his sleeve. He wanted to see change in a society based on tribal voting. He was howling against the wind. The status quo ruled the country. He stared at the reporters with hostility.

"Idiots," he said. "The French take to the barricades to bring down a government. What do we do? Moan and take it up the arse every time. The fighting Irish? Don't make me laugh."

"I think it's called democracy."

"Rule of the people? Who are you kidding? It's rule of the tribe here. Anyway, I'm glad you're off the hook. Have they enough evidence to convict the corpse?"

"I think so."

"Barry Allen wasn't implicated?"

"No, he wasn't."

"He had you beaten up, hadn't he?"

"Over something else."

"Murder must be the only crime he hasn't on his CV, Jack. He has all the rest. Why not? He won't go to jail for perjury. He won't go to jail for taking bribes. Don't they understand? If the law doesn't apply to all, the law applies to none."

I went home with a red ear from listening to Charlie. The whiskey didn't help me sleep. That little girl wouldn't let me sleep. I thought about her mother too. I didn't know what might happen to her. I only knew Carol had suffered more from the death of her twin than anyone else. Maybe she did believe that her twin was reincarnated in her daughter. But that was a case for the State to decide.

By early summer it didn't matter anyway. Hilary Quirke hired a team of expensive lawyers to represent her daughter. They pointed out that Carol was a mother, and that she was entitled to bail on humanitarian grounds. They also pointed out that every person was innocent until proven guilty. Furthermore, she had no previous convictions and therefore was not a danger to the public.

They failed to mention she'd killed Paul Murphy.

She was granted bail and the doctor went guarantor. The court ordered her to surrender her passport. It never occurred to the judiciary that she might have two passports. After all, she did live in France. Carol surrendered her Irish passport and that satisfied the judiciary. It didn't take a genius to figure out what she'd do next because she held a French passport too.

A week after getting bail, a Citroen car was found burnt out in Ballymun, a suburb of the city near the airport. She was missing, and so was her daughter. An alert was sent to France but it was already too late. She'd never be found. The dogs in the street knew that too, if anybody had bothered to ask them.

"The bail laws need tightening up."

I was having lunch with Brady in the centre of the city, over a department store. As far as he was concerned, she shouldn't have been granted bail. I didn't see it his way. Justice had been done in my estimation. Paul Murphy had murdered his wife, the sister of Carol. In return, he had been murdered. These things had a way of balancing themselves out.

"You bailed me out, remember?"

"I'm regretting it now."

"She was Colleen's identical twin, Dermot."

"So what? She took the law into her own hands. That's a recipe for anarchy. That's why they have feuds in countries without a proper justice system. An eye for an eye leaves everyone blind."

He saw it in black and white terms. That logic could be applied to the majority of people, but not to identical twins. They were different. Ordinary rules did not apply to them. If the law didn't take that into account, then the law was wrong.

"By the way, Jack, I'm suspended."

"What for?"

"Discharging a firearm and endangering the public."

"By firing a warning shot in the air?"

"Seems so. I wrote out a report of the incident and Kenny picked it up. He said I had recklessly endangered the public."

"So now I'm the public? That's a compliment."

"Don't thank me, thank Kenny."

"Well, you did fire a shot at a passing cloud."

"Nothing to do that that. He has to take it out on someone for losing that job. Imagine starching his shirt five days a week and not getting rewarded. And him keeping the country safe from every crime possible. What's happening to our beloved land?"

Brady could crack a joke and make it sound serious. He was happy though that Kenny hadn't got the top job. I was willing to bet he wasn't in the minority. Kenny's type was bad for morale.

"Did you examine her revolver?"

A Colt. Unusual to have an American gun here. Our criminals prefer to use Eastern European weapons. Easier to smuggle in by truck. It wasn't used in any crime previously, if that's what you want to know. She's still a murderer, Jack."

"Don't judge until you have an identical twin."

"Another item you can add to your CV. The special relationship between identical twins by Professor Jack Russell. Pity you can't apply your trained mind to horses. You could buy a villa and retire. Speaking of which, you going back to work?"

"Why not? I won't get a State pension when I retire."

"Just asking. Don't jump down my throat."

CHAPTER EIGHTEEN

Next morning at work the phone rang. It was Hilary Quirke. She rang to say thanks for not pressing charges against Carol for the abduction at gunpoint. I suspected she'd helped Carol escape. She'd lost the bail money, but any mother would do that for a daughter she loved. She'd treated Carol as an integral part of her family, not as an intruder.

"She rang to assure me she's fine, and to apologise to you for the whole charade. Carol now realises that she used you, the loss of her twin made her act out of character. She absconded because she could not bear being parted from her daughter."

"And you lost the bail money?"

"A small price to pay for her happiness."

"Sure. I understand. Where is she?"

"I can't answer that question."

The weeks passed and early summer arrived in the city with rainy days and nights. The mind had healed up, and I took to visiting a nearby gym for exercise for the body. A few rounds with aspiring young boxers helped keep me in shape too, sparring sessions. Brady was keeping me informed about the unknown whereabouts of Carol Quirke. She had disappeared from the map of Europe. She knew where to hide and she had enough money to support herself and her daughter. She had salted it away because that's how she operated.

Jane tidied up, clearing her desk before flying off for her summer holidays. She went out to eat and came back with a scowl on her face and a redtop newspaper in her hand. She opened it on my desk, pointing out a picture. I recognised Darren Pringle.

He wore a white wedding suit. I didn't know if he was the groom or the bride because his partner was a man. He was standing to the right of his partner but I didn't know what that signified.

"What do you think of that fucker, Jack?"

"Don't tell me you're jealous."

"Knock it off, you know what I mean."

"Gay marriage is legal here now."

"What the fuck was he doing dating me?"

I didn't say he'd been pumping her for information. She was setting out on a new life with a new beginning. A line had to be drawn under the past and Pringle belonged there.

"Confused about his sexuality maybe."

"The bollix."

She had effectively removed him from her memory with a single swearword. She sat at her desk and punched a few keys on the laptop.

"Should I send a bill to Anne Neary, Jack? You did expose the killer, but then she did a runner. What do you think?"

"No, leave it. She's taken enough hits already."

The phone rang and she answered. A man was

looking for a private detective to tail his wife. She was running around with a younger man who happened to be into older women. He wanted enough proof to kick her out without costing him too much money.

I referred him to Tom Dalton. It was his speciality, not mine. Insurance scams were my line of business. She introduced me to her boyfriend, a shy and respectful young man. They were complete opposites. Maybe that's the way it should be in human relations, one complementing the other. No two people are the same. Not even identical twins are the same. Every person is an individual.

"Take care of her, Eamon."

"I will, sir."

It was a long time since I'd been called that. There was hope for the young after all.

"We're off to Florida tomorrow, Jack. Don't forget."

Jane was holidaying with him on the Florida coast. I sensed they were good for each other. They were starting out on a new phase in life. The episode with Darren Pringle had passed and left her unscathed. It had vanished from her mind with that swearword.

The young can do that because they have short memories. They think of the future and its endless possibilities. They see life in that future, and hope. The young don't think of death.

I picked up the phone and called Amy Reddy.

THE END

20847734R00124

Printed in Great Britain
by Amazon